Sadie's Lament

Andy Roo

Copyright © 2024 by Andy Roo

First paperback edition 2024

Anuci Press edition 2024

www.anuci-press.com

Cover Design by Christy Aldridge

https://grimpoppydesign.carrd.co/

ISBN 979-8-9898048-5-6 (paperback)

ISBN 979-9898048-6-3 (eBook)

CHAPTER ONE

The little girl stumbled to her closet, terrified in the dead of night.

Her eyes hadn't adjusted to the darkness yet, so her shaking arms stretched out before her to avoid bumping any obstacles—she couldn't risk being heard. Her bedroom light switch was only a few feet away, but she didn't reach for that; she wouldn't risk being seen either.

She found the door handle to her closet and gently pulled it open, but stopped short of going in when she remembered something important.

Dolly!

She couldn't hide in her closet without the support of her companion and only sense of comfort—the threadbare rag doll she'd slept with every night she could recall. She tiptoed back to bed, and from under the covers next to her pillow retrieved Dolly. The girl's eyes were adjusting now and she could make out the pigtailed, red threaded hair and the sewn smile on her oldest friend's face. It gave her some relief, even as she trembled with fright.

With Dolly in hand the girl crept back to the closet, freezing in her tracks as another bang sounded in the house. For a moment she thought it was her bedroom door swinging open. It was not. For now, she wouldn't need to face him.

Quietly, she crept into her closet and settled on top of the old wool blanket laid out on the floor, ignoring its irritating itch. She wrapped herself in the half of the blanket she wasn't sitting on, and hoped she'd be hidden from anyone's sight.

Clutching Dolly to her chest, she rocked back and forth. "Everything is fine," she whispered aloud, believing her words would make it so. "It's only a bad dream."

She remembered what her mother had told her once, that it was ok to tell a white lie if it made the other person feel better; because this time she was awake, and the nightmare she faced was painfully real.

If her mom was still here, she'd know what to do. She'd pick her up and tuck her into bed, then sing the song the girl would always fall asleep to. The girl hummed the song now as best she could remember:

Hush now, my baby
Close your eyes and sleep
Hush now, sweet child
You are mine to keep
Hush now, my darling
Tomorrow you can play
Hush now, dear Sadie
I'll be with you every day...

And then her tears were an avalanche—that distant melody bringing as much sadness as solace. She hugged Dolly and imagined her mother next to her, holding her. She imagined how she would sing that lullaby, the one she wrote for her alone. It filled her with sorrow that the words to the song, like the sound of her mother's voice, were becoming fading memories. But she hummed the song again, hearing the words she still remembered, thinking of the mother she'd never forget.

Hush now, my baby
Close your eyes and sleep....

Soon her eyes fluttered, and for a moment, she was floating.

The crashing sound of glass breaking rocked her from her short lived peace. The chaos downstairs was a bad dream she couldn't escape. Just like the night before. The same as countless nights in the past year. Usually she could hum her Mom's song until it was all she heard and in the morning it would be as though nothing happened. But she couldn't hide from the truth forever.

Tonight would be different. She'd summon the strength of her mother, face her fears, and confront the commotion head on.

She leaped up from her curled position on the floor, still gripping Dolly tightly. Her bare feet whispered across the wooden floor as she approached her bedroom door. With a brave heart and quivering hands, she turned the antique door knob and peeked her head through.

The raucous below grew louder. Curses filled the hallways, reverberating against every wall and up the staircase, until it went through her, sending a shiver up her spine. It was her father's voice, but none of his old character.

She flinched at the sound of another loud crash, followed by even more glass breaking. There was nothing stopping her from turning around and flying back to bed. She could throw the covers over herself, dream of her mother, and wake up in the morning as if nothing happened.

Be brave, she imagined her Dolly saying, still gripped in her sweaty palm. *You can face him, it's only your Dad.*

She inched down the stairs, one tiny step at a time, pausing at the end of the landing. The yellow glow of her father's office shone through a crack in the door a few feet ahead of her. Cautiously, she moved forward, careful not to make a sound.

He was talking to himself again. Not mumbles in the way he had when reading his morning paper. This sounded more like a conversation. No. An argument. But she was positive he was alone. She wished he would go back to how he'd been last year when her mother was still around, instead of the frightening figure she was approaching now.

He'd left the door ajar which she peered through, a window into his madness. Her fingers tightened around Dolly as she surveyed the scene before her.

In what seemed like another life she would visit him in this office daily. She'd have the best seat at his mahogany desk, perched atop his lap coloring, while he worked on his research. Her father would sing while he watered the plants, reciting one of her mother's songs which never sounded as pleasant from his lips. He would polish all the trophies and medals he'd won throughout the years until her reflection shone in them. Then come evening she would have them both, father and mother, tuck her into bed.

What she saw now was far removed from the office she grew up in. Mountains of loose paper and pieces of broken glass were scattered across the mahogany and spilled onto the floor she'd once ran barefoot on. The trophies and medals that decorated the shelves were now dull with dust and grime. The plants that flourished by the light of the windows now wilted and yellowed in darkness, left to die. How long had it been since she stepped in there? How bad had things gotten? Would it get any worse?

He sat hunched over his desk with his back facing her. With focused precision he poured a strange brown liquid into a glass tube. It appeared to have the consistency of syrup and reminded her of mother's pancakes as she watched it fill the vial.

His head rose and her breath caught. He turned to face her, glaring as if she was unwelcome.

"Sadie?"

His eyes were almost identical to the ones she'd looked into for nine years, light brown with flecks of gold. The only difference being the deep circles rimming them, dark, like he forgot to sleep for a week.

He set the vial down in a rack that held various colored liquids and peeled off the large industrial gloves he wore, one finger at a time. Sadie trembled as he approached, his body filling the frame as he pulled the door separating them wide open. When he reached out to touch her she pulled back, and then felt a pang of guilt when he recoiled as if he had touched something hot.

"Sadie. Daddy's been working very hard. You know that, right?"

He crouched now so their eyes were level, his expression heavy in desperation. Solemn, she gulped down tears and nodded.

"But I'm so close!" He pinched his thumb and index finger together. "In fact, I think I've done it. We'll find out tomorrow."

His attention drifted as he stared into the space beyond her shoulder. In these moments Sadie felt he was talking to himself.

"I can't sleep, Daddy," she whispered. "I tried singing Mommy's song, but it didn't work."

He considered her and sighed, and with a faint smile he offered his hand to her.

Relieved, Sadie put her small hand into his large one and followed him up the stairs and back to her room. Perhaps there was nothing to be afraid of.

He tucked her under the covers and hummed the song just as he used to, and for a time she was free from her fear. Her eyes fluttered shut as she allowed her body to relax. All was well now. Just like that, she had her Daddy back. And with the lullaby he hummed, she had her Mommy too.

That night her sweet dreams found her. Her mother sat at the grand piano, playing with the fluidity her years as a concert pianist had afforded her. She wore a black, sparkling gown that contrasted with her porcelain skin, but matched her onyx eyes perfectly. She had just returned from a show, a string quartet starring the grand pianist, Marina Fletcher. Sadie had waited up for her because she promised she would play the closing song of the show, the one that gave her chills. Her slender fingers danced across the keys, and Sadie could see the look on her face that reminded her of how a bird appeared when taking flight. Her mother turned to her with the final stroke of the keys. Goosebumps ran up Sadie's arms at the song's finale while her Mom gazed at her; the smile on her face drowned out by the deep sadness in her eyes as if she knew what would happen next.

Sadie stirred awake, her dream drifting away swift as the night had gone. Her thoughts raced as she stared at the ceiling. She missed her mother terribly. She'd never see her again. She missed her father too, though he never left. For the past year she'd watched him struggle. But last night was the first time she allowed herself to see him in earnest. Lost and confused, and forever changed.

A thought of trying to grip a speeding train flicked in her mind; if she could only grab hold, the moments of respite might last longer. It was morning now, so he'd act more or less like himself. But come nightfall....

The aroma of pancakes filled her nose then, and she breathed in the sweet scent. It had been over a year since she enjoyed her once favorite meal, she hoped she wasn't imagining it. She tore out of bed, leaving Dolly to rest among the blankets, and followed her nose.

Downstairs, the sweet scent became stronger. Gleeful, she entered the kitchen where her father pulled out a chair and welcomed her to take a seat. Her eyes danced across the kitchen, squinting at the autumn sunrise from the window above the sink, taking in the oak dining table where her family shared countless meals, the old appliances where her mom often stood, the special mug on the countertop she'd made for her mom at school. She looked at her mother's seat at the table, forever empty, and her heart sank once more.

"Good morning, dear." His smile was genuine as he set a plateful of blueberry pancakes topped with chocolate chips in front of her. Her favorite. Sadie pinched herself to see if she was still dreaming; her sore arm confirmed her wakefulness.

"How are they?" he asked after her first few bites.

"Yum. Tastes like Mommy's."

He chuckled to himself. "She had a way of making the batter smoother. Brilliant scientist, but I can't even recreate my wife's pancake recipe."

Sadie smiled and slowed her eating, wanting to savor every bite. Wanting to relish every second where it was simple to pretend things had gone back to normal. Her heart was as full as her belly and she wished time would still, to have this moment and hold it forever, lest it slip away.

"Sadie?"

The concern in her father's voice interrupted her thoughts. He pulled out a chair beside her and sat down, took off his glasses and cleaned them with his shirt. He always did this when nervous.

Sadie had one mouthful left, but her appetite was gone. Butterflies in her stomach grew, a knotting sensation came over, and she grieved this lovely moment fleeting faster and faster.

"I'm sorry, honey." A heaviness had taken over his voice. "It hasn't been easy this past year. I am so proud of how strong you've been. You are stronger than I am, that's for sure."

Sadie gulped down tears. It had been an awful year. Her prayers that something would change, that *he* would change, had gone unanswered. She didn't think she was strong, but she knew she had to keep trying.

"But I think I've done it. After all these years. All my experiments and research. Last night I made a breakthrough." He pulled something out of the lab coat draped over his chair. "It was perfect timing. I didn't realize how late it was when you asked me to tuck you in last night. I needed that break. Once I got back to my office, I figured it out."

She saw now it was a vial he'd taken from his pocket, filled with the same dark liquid she'd seen in his office the night before. Sunlight pooled in from every window in the house, giving the illusion the liquid was glowing. Out of another pocket, he pulled a needle, and stuck the prick into the vial. Her heart sank as she watched, mesmerized by the mysterious liquid swirling into the syringe. He flicked the needle twice; he'd told her once doing so was to get rid of the air bubbles that were dangerous when injecting patients.

Sadie felt the rush of blood pulsing through her veins, her heartbeat deafening in her skull, pounding against her tiny frame as if desperate to escape. Cold sweat formed on her forehead, clinging to her like ice on metal. She knew this was too good to be true. He was never completely normal after he spent a night being manic. She should have known better. She shouldn't have allowed herself to get her hopes up.

"Daddy, I'm not hungry anymore. I'm gonna play with Dolly." She pushed the chair out, but he pulled it back with his leg, trapping her.

"This is important Sadie. This is for your own good. You can play with Dolly later." His voice was stern, brows knit tight together. He clutched her arm, his grasp firm, and placed it on the table so that her palm faced up. "This will only be a second."

Helpless, she watched as he pulled out a tourniquet and tied it around her bicep. He prodded on her arm until a vein popped up–a fine, pulsing blue line.

"Just a pinch Sadie, and it will all be over."

"Daddy, please," she tried pleading through tears, but he shushed her. He placed the tip of the needle in the crook of her elbow and counted down.

"Three... Two..."

The needle pierced her skin before he got to 'one'.

CHAPTER TWO

She inhaled the smoke from her joint deep into her lungs, trying to forget. Those memories no longer served her, so why did that long forgotten lullaby creep its way in now?

She reached for her phone and put her playlist on shuffle. The song that played was about violence. An apt choice, as violence was a running theme in Sadie's life. Loss? Abandonment? Sadie knew these too, but violence was always her favorite.

"You can choose how you feel," she muttered to herself, repeating the mantra she once read in a self-help book during one of her lowest moments. *So why have I chosen sadness and melancholy?*

She took another deep drag and held the smoke in her lungs. Only when they burned did she exhale. It brought some relief, but the other fire that lived inside of her could not be so easily extinguished.

'Baby it's violence, violence, and I like it like that.' The lyrics sang with a synthetic rhythm that traced along Sadie's body, leaving goose-flesh in its wake.

This is better, Sadie thought, easing into the numbness her high and music provided. The memories from her childhood were gone for now, but they would return. A life of solitude had ensured her darkest recollections would be her closest friends. When her thoughts were at their darkest, a ten mile run at full speed could normally settle her. It hadn't done the trick today, though, hence the hand-rolled joint.

One good thing about Bellewood, Sadie supposed, besides its natural beauty and isolation which she valued above all else, was the abundance of weed. Sadie guessed it would be easy to grow the crop in a forgotten seaside town surrounded by countless acres of forest to one side, and the expansive ocean on the other, which she gazed at now from her one-bedroom apartment balcony.

The sun had just disappeared beyond the horizon, painting the sky in glorious hues of pink and orange. Below, the waters were still, a picture of perfect peace Sadie craved to emulate in herself. She scanned the scene before drinking in every detail: the wooden planks of the seldom used pier, the orange buoy bobbing lazily in the water beyond, and to the north the abandoned waterfront amusement park. At this distance most people wouldn't have seen what she could, but when one's senses were as heightened as Sadie's, distance was rarely a factor.

With her joint spent, she breathed in the mist in the air instead, savoring the salty smell of the sea. Sadie's love of water was a new one, developing only when her father had moved her to Bellewood not one year prior. She'd always lived in nature; before Bellewood, it was in the woods with her father, and before that it was other woods with a larger family. But that was over now.

She pushed the thoughts away as she always did when they reared. A past as hard and heavy as hers could never be forgotten, but it would drive a person mad to dwell on such things.

Later, when darkness had encroached around her and the music was no longer loud enough to lose herself in, Sadie threw on her leather jacket and set out into the unseasonably cool Bellewood night.

The coastal Bellewood was always quiet at this time, especially this far away from the downtown core.

The town had been settled almost two centuries earlier, when the prospect of striking gold attracted ambitious businessmen from all parts of the country. When their mining efforts failed to yield, enamorment of the site's natural beauty became the reason to stay. So they built their mansions there, each as grandiose as the next. Bellewood became their haven, a home where men could leave their families as they went to the cities to manage both their businesses and their mistresses. A generous allowance permitted their loved ones to fend for themselves in the gorgeous, boring town of Bellewood. Generations later, little had changed. Attempts to develop and revitalize the town—such as the amusement park Sadie passed by now—had failed. The rich were above such childish distractions.

Next to the park's long shuttered gates was a statue of a woman in a flowing dress. The statue must have been at least one hundred years old, and in the darkness and eerie silence she looked like something haunted, her facial features frozen with tortured emotion. Past the gates, an old wooden ferris wheel creaked as if in invitation for Sadie to enter the park.

One day, Sadie promised. She hadn't met a single locked gate that could stop her yet.

Past the park, Sadie continued her trek through nothingness on the boardwalk, the sea her only companion, until a distant sound, carried on the water, reached her.

Low murmurings.

Sadie stopped and listened.

Men, murmuring over an electropop tune.

Sadie continued walking and came face to face with the source of the noise.

Three young men, a little older than Sadie, stood beside a gleaming blue BMW. They passed around a bottle. *Whiskey,* Sadie thought, judging by the faintest scent. They told crude jokes and laughed with delight at their cleverness when they noticed her. Sadie's sudden appearance must have startled them, for all three went quiet, staring in drunken confusion. It was clear they weren't used to encountering anyone out here.

Sadie wasn't bothered. She barely paid them a glance as she walked past, though she did wonder if the long, black hair curtaining and covering her face made her look menacing or meek. When they thought she was out of ear-shot they began talking about her. Some of it was amusing, one of them thought she looked like a vampire. Most of what they said was the typical drivel men spoke when they thought she couldn't hear. Though they whispered, Sadie always heard every word. And then their voices were replaced by their footsteps as they followed behind her.

Idiots, Sadie thought. Whatever it was they had planned, it wouldn't end well for them.

When their steps grew nearer she turned around to face them head-on, letting them know she was aware they were following her. The man in the middle, the alpha fool, had a smug look on his face, as if he was proud of whatever it was he thought he was about to do. The one to his right chuckled, encouraging the one in the middle as he blew a kiss in Sadie's direction. Sadie would make sure he got hurt the worst. Only one of the men looked nervous. Sadie guessed he was the one who thought she looked like a vampire.

If you only knew. I'm so much worse.

The song she'd been listening to earlier replayed in her mind.

'Violence, violence, and I like it like that.'

And so she did.

CHAPTER THREE

Her fists ached, bruised by the pounding she'd delivered a few minutes prior to that group of brutes who definitely deserved it. No matter. The whiskey she had taken from them burned down her throat and would soon numb the pain.

Other than her hands, she didn't have a scratch on her. It was more than those idiots would be able to say. Whenever they woke, after nursing the concussions she doubtlessly delivered along with the black eyes and bloody lips, they'd surely think again before harassing another girl.

Sadie finished what was left of the whiskey when she reached the town center and stepped onto Main Street. She passed a cafe, a pharmacy, a small grocer, and a post office—all closed for the night and eerie in their stillness. But as soon as she walked through the graffiti spangled alleyway off Main Street, it was as if she was in a different city altogether.

Music boomed as she surveyed the scene around her like an extra on a movie set. Young couples walked hand-in-hand, and a group of girlfriends stumbled out of a Porsche wearing heels they hadn't learned to walk in, all rushing to get to their favorite restaurant or lounge, which the strip boasted many of.

Sadie disposed of the empty bottle and walked with elation to the source of the loudest music. She'd never gone out dancing in Belle-wood's infamous nightlife before, but the thoughts she was trying to bury coupled with the intoxicants running through her bloodstream made good enough excuses to try something new.

The exterior of the building she approached was covered in splashes of blue UV paint, and up and down the brick walls were pinpricks of purple LED lights, pulsing in and out.

"ID?" A big bear of a man asked as she approached the club door.

Shit...about that... At eighteen, Sadie was still underage, but that hadn't seemed to ever stop her classmates whom she always overheard talking about blacking out at the clubs.

"Whatever," the man said, bored at Sadie's lack of response. He swung open the large metal door to the club and ushered her through. "Don't do anything stupid in there."

Inside, a large neon sign read *Oxygen Nightclub*; it hung above a small coat-check room where a young woman donned in elaborate black clothing and dark makeup was seated. Sadie eyed the corset the woman was wearing, it was cut low and cropped high, the sequins and carefully placed crystals reflected the purple glow of the neon light, and looked like tiny shimmering galaxies.

"Thanks for staring," the young woman said. "Can I take your coat?"

Sadie could see now that she was about the same age as the coat-check girl, who was absolutely stunning. Her feline eyes were exaggerated with black eyeliner, and her full lips were curved into a smile.

"Unless there was something else you wanted to give me?" She leaned in at this and made a sexy pout, her lips painted black.

Even half-drunk and still a little high, Sadie could tell she was being flirted with. She felt her cheeks grow warm, and hoped it was dark enough so the girl couldn't see how stupid she must have looked.

"Uh, n-no thanks," Sadie replied sheepishly. "I'll keep my jacket on."

The girl shrugged and gave her one more smile as Sadie walked toward the dance floor.

The club was dark, save for a deep, pulsating red light that vibrated in sync with her heart. A large television was set over a stage, playing the *Dracula* series. Standing on stage was a DJ. His hair was shaved on the sides, but long and straight on top, dyed purple and sweeping over his left shoulder. He was adorned in beautiful, dark, vintage clothing that matched his eyeliner and the spider web tattooed on his cheek. The music he played was ominous, yet seductive, like the club's ambience.

The dance floor was packed for a weeknight, and everyone seemed to be dressed in similar clothing. It was as if the pastel-painted walls of Bellewood had been knocked down and replaced with crimson velvet blouses and black combat boots. She glanced around the club with elation. For the first time since arriving in Bellewood she could easily relax into the crowd without standing out.

She made her way to the middle of the dance floor, which was un-characteristic of her, proof that the whiskey was working. The music picked up as if on cue. Her heart matched its pace, and before she knew it her hips swayed to the rhythm of the synth tunes.

Sadie had never danced in public before, so she was sure she wasn't good at it, but she allowed herself to feel the beat and move with the rhythm anyway, euphoric that she was finally feeling *something*. The pandemonium of her life seeped out of her mind and pores, and dripped onto the dance floor.

Other dancers encircled her as if in answer to her siren's call. Some wore masks, and Sadie guessed they were beautiful behind them. They were all one with the music, lost in ecstasy, hands in the air in celebration of their youth, bodies twisting and turning, seduced by the permeating rhythm. And Sadie was one with them. Surrounded by people just like her, when all her life she'd been so alone.

After a few more songs Sadie worked up a sweat, and regretted her choice not to hand over her jacket to the girl at coat-check. But, as though summoned, Sadie watched the girl approach her, hips swaying in a mesmerizing melody with the music, her feline eyes staring deep inside her.

"I guessed whiskey on the rocks," she yelled over the music, and handed Sadie a drink.

Sadie felt the rush of blood to her cheeks again as she accepted the drink and took a generous gulp. "How'd you guess?"

"You just seem like my type of girl," she replied, her voice a deep hum, splitting through the synth pop pulsing through the club, and it somehow vanished. All that remained were this stranger's voice, and her own pounding heart. Coat-check girl eyed Sadie up and down, her pouting lips forming a half smile. "So...I was right then?"

Sadie felt like she swallowed a hundred moths. Why was this girl talking to her when she must look like a sweaty, soppy mess? A gorgeous girl at that. All Sadie could manage was awkward bewilderment, so she simply took another sip and walked to the edge of the dance floor, away from the crowd.

The girl followed. "Not one for small talk? That's fine, I like the quiet type. My name's Destiny, what's yours?"

"Is that your real name?" The words came out harsher than Sadie had intended, and she bit her lip in embarrassment.

Destiny laughed and pushed a lock of sweaty hair behind Sadie's ear. "I think so. That's what it says on my ID, anyway." She pulled out a wallet from her rear pocket.

Sadie's attention was drawn to her waist and how perfect her jeans sat on her body. The leanness of her shoulders and the definition of her stomach reminded her of a swimmer. She was a certified vixen, and she was making Sadie nervous.

"See?"

Distracted, Sadie pulled her attention to the ID held in front of her. A student card with a photograph and name. Sure enough, in bold black letters, the name DESTINY YU stared back at her.

"You go to Bellewood Prep?" Sadie asked. There was only one high school in Bellewood—private, due to the generations of inherited, unfathomable wealth—which Sadie attended. She'd never seen Destiny before, but Sadie had only started at Bellewood Prep in the start of senior year, so she was unfamiliar with most of the student body.

"Senior year." Destiny nodded. "You looked kind of familiar, so I came to say hi."

This was a surprise. Sadie had spent so much time trying to go unnoticed, for anyone besides her one and only friend to approach her was rare. It wasn't unheard of, but when it happened it was usually due to a combination of morbid curiosity and hateful vitriol.

"I *was* kind of checking you out if that's what you were thinking," Destiny said when Sadie stayed silent. "The way you were moving out there was really hot. You were completely enveloped in the song, like it was just you out there. You were in your own little world, and I have to admit, I wanted a tour."

Sadie took another nervous swig of her drink, and despite her best efforts, could not maintain eye contact with Destiny. *Her eyes are gorgeous, though...* Destiny was sexy, charismatic, confident. She was everything Sadie wasn't, though for the first time tonight, thought she could be. *Wanted* to be. She imagined this is how it would feel to be like everyone else in Bellewood.

"You're Olivia's friend, right?" Destiny asked with a tilt of her head, her brown hair reaching the top of her cleavage.

The beat of a new song shook the walls.

"Do you stalk me or something?" Sadie could feel her defenses rising, uncomfortable by the attention she was getting, even if it was from a sultry stranger.

"Is that an invitation?" Destiny asked, taking a step closer.

Sadie didn't feel herself take a step back until she collided with someone who responded to her apology with a scowl. Embarrassed, she returned her gaze to Destiny, who was smiling at her.

"So?" Destiny asked, searching Sadie with her eyes.

Enough of this, Sadie thought. She downed the rest of her drink and handed the empty glass to Destiny. "The only thing you're invited to do," Sadie said, "is get me another one of these."

"You're bossy." Destiny took the empty glass from her. "I think that's *so* sexy."

Destiny's eyes swept over Sadie's body and she felt her cheeks flush for the third time that night.

"I'll be right back. Keep dancing!" Destiny said, before turning and making her way toward the bar.

Sadie watched as she walked away, her jeans complementing her generous derrière. Destiny's exposed lower back revealed a floral tattoo, vibrant against her tanned skin and tight core. *Am I seriously checking another girl out right now? How drunk* am *I?*

Seated at the bar a few paces from where Destiny stood was a guy Sadie had never seen before, but somehow he stood out from the crowd. The first thing she noticed about him was that he was wearing a black leather jacket, just like her. The next was that he was staring at her, his emerald eyes piercing hers, setting those moths in her stomach into a frenzied flight again. After just a few moments of eye-contact, he stood up, and Sadie was worried he would approach her; she was sure she couldn't handle two people flirting in one night. Instead, he made his way to the exit, and Sadie's eyes lingered on him the whole way.

"You know Dante?" The unexpected voice made Sadie jump. Destiny had returned and caught the last vestiges of their exchange.

"Thanks," Sadie said, receiving her drink. "Dante? That's his name?"

"Yup, he used to go to Bellewood Prep. You still haven't told me *your* name, by the way."

Sadie laughed, embarrassed. "It's Sadie."

"It's been a pleasure meeting you tonight, Sadie." Her voice was a purr, and Sadie shuddered. "But I should get back to work. I'll see you around, I hope." Destiny gave one last wink before departing, leaving Sadie alone on the dance floor.

By now, something had shifted and Sadie was no longer in a dancing mood, but her mission for the night was accomplished. She was finally calm, tired, and even a little bit happy, if not entirely too drunk. Still, she downed the drink Destiny had brought her before deciding to go home. She may have stumbled slightly on her way off the dance floor, but she didn't think anyone noticed.

As slyly as she could, she turned to the coat check room to see if Destiny was watching as she left, as she'd done to Dante. What she saw instead was a couple of men in their twenties hand Destiny some rolled up bills. Destiny pocketed the money, and rather than handing the men their coats, she passed them something in a closed fist, too small to see. Just as fast as the transaction was, the men put whatever it was in their mouths and swallowed.

Sadie had no idea what Destiny's story was, but it seemed there were a few more well kept secrets hiding in Bellewood than she previously thought.

She left the club, thanking the bouncer as she exited, and he grunted in response.

Cool air greeted her, which she was thankful for. She hadn't realized how warm it was inside. Standing a few feet from her, leaning against the brick exterior of the club and smoking a joint, was the handsome boy she'd seen inside.

Dante.

Noticing Sadie staring, he exhaled the smoke, and gestured with his joint, inviting her to smoke with him.

On any other night, she would have ignored him. On any other night, she would have turned and walked away. Tonight, she felt drawn toward him. There was something magnetizing about his aura. He was cool and dark, which was perfect, as Sadie was always on the hunt for a distraction from her even colder and darker thoughts.

She took the joint from his hand and inhaled, deep and slow.

Dante's weed was grades above what she was used to smoking, and she held the smoke in, savoring the more pleasant taste for a little too long before exhaling. He seemed to find it funny, his chuckle throaty and hoarse, his eyes a bemused gleam of curiosity.

"Having a good night?" he asked. His voice was deep, his tone carefree. The smirk he wore suggested he didn't care if she'd had a good night or not. Still, he was pleasant enough.

"Better now," Sadie said, taking another drag.

He grinned, and Sadie took note of how gorgeous his mouth was. Beautiful lips, perfect teeth. The cutest single dimple nestled his left cheek, adding to the allure of his smile.

"Oh yeah? Why's that?" Dante asked.

Sadie realized it wasn't just his mouth she found gorgeous. His eyes gleamed that emerald-green again, shining on his sun-kissed skin. Messy, brown hair, styled that way with care, fell across one eye, his stare piercing her. Beneath his leather jacket Sadie could guess at his perfect physique.

Because you're here, she thought, though she was sober enough to keep from saying it. Instead she shrugged, passed him the joint. "Just having a good night is all."

"I bet," Dante said, and he took a long inhale. The smoke billowed around them, thick and sweet with a hint of blueberry, and she stepped closer into it. "Are you all right?" he asked, laughing, taking a step back.

"Never better," she answered, and fixed him with a stare she hoped he'd find as sexy as she found him.

He glared at her, curiosity bleeding from him, and she retreated, self-conscious. She realized she was out of it—the weed wasn't mixing well with the whiskey—and was probably making a fool of herself. But Dante was...

"So sexy," she thought aloud.

He burst out laughing. "Thanks... Yeah, you too."

Widening her eyes, her cheeks burning, Sadie avoided his gaze, desperate for a reason to run the hell away.

"I'd love to hang out, but my ride's here." Dante took one last drag before passing the joint to Sadie. "Here, why don't you finish the rest of this. I'll see you around."

Without looking back, Dante disappeared into the back of a brand new, black Mercedes sedan.

Despite her embarrassment, she felt disappointed, but wouldn't let it show. All she could do now was watch him drive away.

CHAPTER FOUR

Bellewood Prep sat at the precipice of the Bellewood Bluffs overlooking Crescent Bay. On days when the tide was high, as at present, you could get sprayed with sea water from the student parking lot, all the way to the football field on the other side of campus. The crashing waves and seagulls' cries echoed throughout the whole school, and nearly every window offered a breath-taking view of the ocean, reflecting the early spring's clear-sky, sunny day. The school was a beacon in the community from the cliff on which it stood. From the vast Coquette Woods in the north-east to the town in the south-east, Bellewood Prep was the one modern structure in a small, seaside town where everything, including the money, was old. The school housed state-of-the-art facilities and technology, and among the student body were some of Bellewood's youngest and brightest citizens, if not the richest and most spoiled.

The school was revered as the 'Academic Jewel' of the southwest for young adults according to an article Sadie's father had found when he'd registered her as a senior before moving her to Bellewood. But on her first day she had already expected the stares, whispers, and jests at her expense. Sadie Fletcher's place in the mix was the same as all her past schools–the ostracized outcast. Despite its high honors and exclusivity, Bellewood Prep did not differ from any other school.

Sadie pressed her forehead into her locker door. The coldness of the metal was a relief to the pounding in her head due to the hangover she was nursing. Luckily Sadie had a free first period every morning which allowed her to sleep in, but that did little to help her today after she'd stayed up most of the night at Oxygen Nightclub. In history class, Mr. Ramirez had to wake Sadie up twice before finally giving up and letting her sleep the rest of second period. Then in English class, the Shakespeare reading was a perfect lullaby, but Ms. Mora would sooner bite Sadie's head off then allow her a nap. Now in the moments before final period the halls were filled with excited chatter, and every high pitched voice was like glass, stabbing Sadie's brain.

"There you are!" Olivia Baltimore squealed.

"Sssh. Not so loud, *please*," Sadie said, but smiled as her friend linked her arm through hers.

They met on Sadie's first day at Bellewood Prep. She'd assumed her experience at this school would be the same as all the rest; that the other girls would judge her as weird before getting to know her, and that the guys would only talk to her in a bid to get her into bed. Still, she allowed herself some hope on that first day that this time would be different. It was not. Sadie heard the whispered words of judgment from her peers as she walked the halls alone, lost. And once the popular guys tried hitting on her despite her disinterest, it was over; the territorial mean girls had made up their mind that she would never be welcome. All except for Olivia Baltimore. On that first day, Olivia had sat across from Sadie and introduced herself. When Sadie stayed quiet, Olivia said that was for the best, because she could do enough talking for the both of them. From that day on they were friends. Olivia had quickly broken through Sadie's wall, and stayed true to her, even as the other girls did their best to turn Olivia against her.

"It's seriously messed up how we only have final period together this semester," Olivia said, not hearing Sadie's request to speak quietly. While she had a heart of gold, Olivia did far more talking than listening. Sadie didn't mind though, she preferred it that way.

"Ohmygod!" Olivia exclaimed even louder than before. "You will not believe what happened at lunch."

Besides me sneaking into an empty classroom to sleep off this hangover and waking up feeling worse?

"A deputy at the police department called me back!"

"Is that a good thing?" Sadie asked, apprehensive. She immediately went through the mental rolodex of illegal activity she'd committed recently, beating up those thugs on the coast sticking out most of all.

"You know that Bellewood drug problem?" Olivia asked in a way that suggested everyone knew.

"No?" Sadie replied, confused.

Olivia gave a dramatic, disapproving sigh before explaining that recent news stories of rampant drug use and overdoses in Bellewood was a new phenomenon that had all started within the last few months. She went on to explain that the situation was getting worse, with more and more people—including students at Bellewood Prep—getting high on this new drug called *Bliss*.

Sadie thought of Destiny then—she was sure she'd seen her sell something to those guys right before she left the club.

"Anyway," Olivia went on, "someone from the police department is supposed to get back to me in a couple of days for an exclusive interview for the school paper. Isn't that great?"

There were a few things about Olivia that Sadie knew for sure. First, she was by far the best human being at the school—if not the world—and second, she was never as serious about *anything* as her role of school newspaper editor. Olivia thrived on peeling back layers of a story, no matter what it was, and if it happened to be juicy enough, putting it on the cover of the next monthly issue. Olivia's stories had grown in popularity since she took over as editor, so that teachers and students alike would stop her in the halls to congratulate her on her work and research, and to discuss ways they could help in whatever topic Olivia was most passionate about that month. Well, as long as it didn't expose their own sordid privacy.

Sadie wanted to be supportive of her friend, but she had a bad feeling about this. She knew drugs could be dangerous business, and she'd hate to see Olivia get messed up in something dark. She was the sweetest person Sadie had ever known; her bouncing blonde curls, big blue eyes, and rosy cheeks all added to her innocence.

They headed to their class together, Olivia chatting on about something-or-other, while Sadie fielded angry glares from passersby. Olivia had once sworn to Sadie that they only stared because she was so pretty. Why so hateful then? Olivia's answer had been that they were jealous. Sadie knew her friend was just being kind, though. The fact was Bellewood Prep was not a welcoming place to outsiders, least of all outsiders who made no effort to fit in.

They reached class just as the bell rang and rushed to their seats at the back of the room. Ms. Petrelli was known for handing out after school detentions for latecomers, but as luck would have it, she herself was late. Naturally, the class separated into their friend groups to enjoy a chat before the teacher arrived.

Sadie did her best to ignore the whispers and giggles at her expense from the mean girls at the front of the class: Claire Gostosi and her lackey, Bree Huxley. But as usual, she couldn't unhear their whispers.

"Such a freak!" Claire murmured as she stared straight at Sadie with a look of disdain. "Why does Olivia sit with her, anyway? She should be sitting with us."

"They can have each other," Bree whispered, and then stole a glance at the boy beside her, Joaquin Hernandez, Olivia's ex-boyfriend.

Sadie was grateful to have Olivia beside her to distract her, but for once, Olivia was silent. Her eyes were fixed on Brock Banner. Tall, athletic, and handsome, Brock was best friends with Joaquin who Olivia had dated all junior year, a fact Olivia didn't seem to mind.

When she was finished staring, Olivia turned her attention to Sadie. "So you're coming to Brock's party tonight right? No excuses!"

About that... Sadie had every intention to go straight home after school and sleep off her wicked hangover, but she knew how persistent her friend could be.

"All seniors are invited," Olivia continued, "and Brock has the *best* party house. Both his parents are out of town on business, so we'll have the place to ourselves... And who knows, you might meet someone cute!"

Sadie's thoughts went to Dante from last night. What were the odds of that gorgeous young man attending a high school party?

"Do you know someone named Dante?" Sadie asked before she could stop herself.

Olivia lit up like a tree on Christmas morning. "Dante Nerosi?" She couldn't contain her excitement, and Sadie had to look around to make sure no one was listening in. "He used to go here, graduated a couple years ago. He's *cute*! You know him?"

"I guess so? We met last night," Sadie said. What she didn't say was how he had kind of told her he found her sexy. Granted, she'd said it first, but that wasn't the point.

"Well you *have* to come to the party then!" Olivia demanded. "Brock and him are friends. Maybe he'll show up!"

Suddenly the thought of going to Brock's senior party didn't seem like the worst idea to Sadie. She was thinking of Dante's green eyes again, and his dimpled smile. Getting a second chance at running into him was a pleasant idea, especially if she could manage to not make a fool of herself.

Olivia was still talking about all the reasons why Brock's party was going to be the best, when Sadie heard something distressing from outside the classroom. It sounded like a gasp followed by several adult voices whispering frantically to each other. Sadie could have sworn she heard the word *murder* being thrown around from the hallway.

"What's wrong, Sadie?" Olivia asked.

Sadie's face must have betrayed her. For her entire life, Sadie had to remind herself that she wasn't like other people. She could see from distances others couldn't, and hear things coming from several rooms away, where no one else was the wiser. Her enhanced senses were a gift as well as a curse—one she had to keep hidden from all who knew her, as her father would always tell her.

"Nothing's wrong," Sadie lied. "Just tired I guess."

After a moment, Ms. Petrelli entered the classroom. The students took their seats and settled down on her arrival. Right away Sadie noticed the teacher's face was contorted in a scowl, and she looked queasy, like she was about to be sick.

"Class, I'm afraid I have some terrible news." Ms. Petrelli's voice came out shaking, and though she tried to fight it, a sob escaped her. "Something awful has happened."

The class broke into murmurs. Some wondered if their teacher was joking, others dreaded what she would say next.

Ms. Petrelli was bawling now. "One of our beloved students...has been found...dead"—she gasped at the word and steeled herself to continue—"on the north side of the coast. Her name was Katie Phillips, a junior. For now, there aren't many details...but police are saying she was—" Her voice broke, her lips trembled. "Murdered."

The class erupted in gasps and shrieks. Some had known Katie well.

"The police are warning everyone to be extra careful," Ms. Petrelli continued, trying to speak over the chaos. "There is no suspect yet, so the murderer is still on the loose. They say it was a vicious attack."

Claire broke down in hysterical sobs. She was either the most upset by the news, or simply pretending to be by putting on a full show of it. Ms. Petrelli walked toward her and laid a comforting hand on her shoulder.

"Until further notice, classes are cancelled," the teacher announced. "Everybody is to go home with a buddy, and under no circumstances should you go anywhere alone."

All Sadie could think about were the three thugs she'd encountered on the shore the night before. They had been out there looking for trouble. Did they find it before Sadie had knocked them unconscious? Had she gone too easy on them?

Beside her, Olivia had gone pale, but even so, she pulled out a notepad, furious scribbles filling the page—the beginnings of a new article.

Sadie shivered. It was as though her friend was insisting on getting herself into a dangerous situation. *What will I need to do to keep her safe?*

CHAPTER FIVE

"Are you sure going to this party is still a good idea?"

"Believe me, I hate this as much as you do," Olivia replied.

Sadie somehow doubted that, even though her friend seemed sincere. They were sitting in Olivia's bed in her parents' mansion in East Hills, the fancy part of town. Olivia had insisted that they do the buddy system, like Ms. Petrelli suggested, and go home together. Olivia knew Sadie lived alone in her one-bedroom apartment on the outskirts of town, and refused to let her be alone tonight.

"But yes, we should still go to Brock's party," Olivia said. "The killer might be there."

"*How* can that be a good thing?" Best friend or not, Olivia never failed to perplex her.

"It is if they get exposed, and we get some justice for Katie. Her *heart*, Sadie. What kind of monster would do such a thing?"

Several hours had passed since school was let out early, and by now rumors were being thrown around left and right as to what happened to Katie.

"We don't know it was her heart," Sadie said. "We don't know anything yet."

What could be agreed upon was that Katie was found on the shore of Bellewood Beach, even though she lived in the East Hills part of town which was a few miles away. That in itself wasn't odd, the beach was always a popular hangout for Bellewood teens, even in colder weather. But the latest rumor being accepted as true was that the killer destroyed Katie's face, and then removed her heart, leaving a faceless, heartless corpse behind. Some people speculated a jealous ex-boyfriend. But those who knew her said her ex lived out of state, and that there wasn't anyone in her life who was angry enough with her to do such a thing.

"Something strange is going on in Bellewood, Sadie." Olivia sprang from the four-poster bed, and paced her large bedroom. The walls were a pale pink color, a remnant from childhood, but were mostly covered with bookcases housing hardcover crime novels. "This has never been the perfect town," Olivia continued. "The kids have no supervision and more money than they can possibly spend, and there are more narcissists living here than I can count, but this has always been a *boring* place to live. Not much has ever happened. Then this drug problem making waves in the last few months, and now this vicious murder? Sadie, what if the two are related?"

"Drugs and violence do go hand in hand, I guess?" Her voice betrayed her skepticism.

"I'd never peg her for the type, but what if Katie had gotten involved with some sketchy people? A drug deal gone wrong?"

"I don't know," Sadie doubted. "To tear the girl's face off and heart out? It seems a lot more personal than that.

Olivia shivered at the thought. "Whatever it is, we need to get to the bottom of it."

Sadie could not agree less with this logic, but even if she did want 'to get to the bottom of it,' she doubted they'd be able to if they were inebriated; Olivia was now pouring two large glasses of wine from the bottle she'd snatched from her parents' bar downstairs.

"What?" Olivia asked innocently. "It will settle our nerves."

\#

Darkness shrouded them as they walked up Brock's expansive driveway. The Tesla Uber Olivia had ordered dropped them off at Brock's mansion's front gates, but there was still a couple minutes walk to the house from there.

Olivia glanced over each shoulder, and then again; shadows creeping in like tendrils in the dead of night. Her fear was understandable, but she was safe with Sadie. If there was a killer lurking, and if he was stupid enough to attack Sadie *or* Olivia, Sadie would make him suffer.

"Relax, you're in good company," was all Sadie said, even though she looked like a hooker. After a few glasses of wine she'd allowed Olivia to dress her. It wasn't bad enough that the tiny dress she wore rose higher up her legs with each footstep, her feet also ached, squeezed into a too small pair of stilettos. If she made it through the night, Sadie swore to never borrow Olivia's clothes again.

Booming music greeted them when they reached the house's double oak wood doors. The party seemed to be well underway by the sounds of it. Brock answered the door after Olivia rang the bell, and the music and laughter spilled through the entrance.

"Hi, Brock!" Olivia chirped.

He looked at the girls with half-drunk smugness, his eyes scanning over their attire, drinking in the sight.

"Well, well," he drawled. "Olivia Baltimore & Sadie Fletcher at *my* party?"

Olivia giggled like a fangirl, clearly smitten by the definition of his muscles in his tight pink polo. Sadie rolled her eyes at his obvious self-righteousness, but he didn't notice.

He gestured the girls inside, told them to make themselves at home while he got them a drink before disappearing into the mix of dancing teenage bodies.

The grandiosity of Brock's home rendered the girls speechless. The main foyer was large enough to be Sadie's apartment and the floors were white marble as far as they could see. A striking chandelier with countless sparkling crystal pendants hung from the ceiling, giving the impression of a waterfall made of diamonds, and at the foot of the stairs was professional DJ equipment connected to several speakers that blared music throughout the house.

"Is that Mitchell?" Olivia shouted to be heard over the music. She grabbed Sadie's hand and dragged her further inside where they spotted a lanky guy sporting a Marvel Comics t-shirt talking to a group of girls. There was no denying the bright green framed glasses and the messy brown mop he called hair on top of his head.

Sadie chuckled at the sight, even as she envied what he was wearing, pulling on her dress again. She was surprised to see Mitchell Carmichael at this party, though she hardly went to parties enough herself to know if he was the type. He was kind and goofy, and entirely too geeky, though not unattractive. But other than occasionally hanging out with Sadie and Olivia, he mostly kept to himself. Which was why Sadie was surprised to see him surrounded by a group of girls, chatting like they were old friends. She was even more surprised to realize that one of those girls was Destiny Yu, the young woman she met at Oxygen Nightclub. Olivia's warning played out in Sadie's mind again—the Bellewood drug problem. Was Mitchell getting involved in something seedy? Was there potential for danger?

When Mitchell saw Sadie and Olivia at the doorway staring at him, he shot them a happy grin, said something to Destiny, and walked toward them.

Sadie tried to catch Destiny's eye but she was involved in another conversation now.

Another customer?

"You guys made it!" Mitchell exclaimed when he reached them, and pulled them into a bearhug.

"Ew, get off," Olivia protested as Sadie laughed. Olivia and Mitchell had known each other for years, which led her to treat him like an annoying brother. Sadie was nice to him because he was a harmless sweetheart.

"I'm so *happy* to see you," Mitchell slurred. Sadie could tell he'd been drinking which also surprised her.

"Please don't tell me you were talking to Destiny Yu," Olivia said to him.

"What? She seems cool!"

From Olivia's tone, Sadie knew better than to admit she'd hung out with Destiny the night before and had also thought she was cool.

"If you consider selling drugs *cool*," Olivia said, disapproval evident with each syllable.

So she was *selling drugs at Oxygen,* Sadie thought.

"What? You think Destiny's responsible for all the drugs coming through Bellewood?" Mitchell said. "No way!"

"That's what I've heard," Olivia said, challenging him. "I've been doing my research, remember? And in the seniors group chat tonight a few of the guys were making comments about Destiny being the go-to girl '*if you want to party*'. It's not hard to guess what that's supposed to mean."

They argued back and forth about their conspiracy theories of what kind of girl Destiny was. Sadie didn't dare confirm she saw Destiny in what she was almost positive was a drug sale the night before. Whatever Destiny was into, and however Olivia felt about it, that was one drama Sadie did not want to involve herself in.

Brock returned with drinks for himself and Olivia, evidently forgetting to offer Sadie one. Mitchell complained that his cup was empty and stalked off in search of another round. Olivia tossed half her drink back in one go, giggling at whatever nonsense Brock was talking about.

It was a little known secret that Olivia had somewhat of a massive crush on Brock, which wasn't hard considering he stood tall at well over six feet and had the physique of a Greek God. But it was never so obvious as now that Olivia had some liquid courage in her. Sadie was glad to see it, Olivia hadn't dated anyone since her loser ex cheated on her, and it was time for her to move on. So to give them some privacy and stop being a massive third wheel, Sadie left Brock and Olivia, and wandered aimlessly through the house.

The house stretched forever, and there were people in every chamber and hallway she passed. Down a set of stairs, Sadie had encountered the most lavish indoor pool oasis she'd ever seen. It was the *only* indoor pool oasis she'd ever seen. Modern sun chairs with lush white cushions lined one side of the pool, while a waterfall made of rocks cascaded onto a couple locked in an embrace. The entire floor and pool were tiled with gray stones, and the dim lighting and collection of potted exotic plants made it look like a tropical underground cave.

She slipped out of her heels, and her toes were instantly grateful. She had thought to put her feet in the pool, until she noticed the Queen of Mean, Claire Gostosi, in a tiny bikini seated at the edge of the water. A few guys who Sadie recognized as being from the football team had their arms draped on the edge smiling as they faced her. Claire playfully kicked her legs in the pool, splashing them and herself as they laughed in unison. Sadie suddenly felt her dinner wanting to come up. The couple under the waterfall, Sadie now realized, was Joaquin and Bree—Olivia's ex and the girl he cheated with.

You dodged a bullet, Olivia.

Even though it had been a few months, Olivia was still not completely over the betrayal. Sadie could have killed the jerk for breaking her best friend's heart.

Sadie exited the pool room unseen, and wandered the remainder of the mansion alone, gradually getting farther away from the sounds of the party.

One quiet room led to another, and then through French chateau doors, Sadie found herself in the garden. The spades of tulips and hydrangeas she recognized, but the other plants and flowers screamed luxury. She was sure she was too poor to have ever seen plants so magnificent.

Sadie was so enamored by the garden, she didn't even notice the man standing there, watching her.

Until he reached out and grabbed her.

CHAPTER SIX

If she was more impulsive, she could have broken his neck. One swift hit, placed with precision, was all it would take. Lucky for him, she paced herself, for she now recognized the piercing green eyes staring back at her.

Dante Nerosi.

"Did I frighten you?" His voice was butter, rich and smooth. It might have been the wine talking, but the way he looked, bright green eyes over tanned skin, brown curls, and a mischievous grin dimpling his cheek made her mind run wild with obscene thoughts.

Sadie realized she was close to drooling, but got it together quick. "Do you always lurk in the bushes like a creep?" She couldn't appear too interested. She'd learned from last time.

He laughed and looked to the ground, embarrassed. Sadie could get used to gorgeous men being humble.

"No. Well, yes. I was trying to get away from the party. I didn't mean to scare you when I touched your arm, but we haven't been properly introduced yet."

Gorgeous or not, Sadie was still unsure of this guy, and contemplated going back to the party to find her friends. But when he put out his hand and gave her his name, she reciprocated, leaving out the fact she already knew his name, so as to not scare him off.

He held her hand longer than he had to, his touch soft and warm as his eyes peered into hers. She thought she might blush or drool, or do any number of things that might embarrass herself again, but she refused to do so.

When the eye contact became too much, he looked away first, a shy smile spread across his face, and Sadie found him even more attractive then.

"I'm glad to see you here," he said. "After last night, I was worried we wouldn't get the chance. But it must be my lucky day to see you twice in twenty-four hours."

Sadie was half drunk *and* had a hangover, a girl had just been viciously murdered, and Olivia was sticking her nose in places that could get her in trouble. She wouldn't have described the last twenty-four hours as lucky, but at least it was working out for Dante.

"I'm glad to see you too," Sadie said, even if this exchange was way too awkward, since she'd had far less to drink compared to last night.

"So what are you doing out here?" Dante asked, stepping closer to her. "All alone..."

"I came with a friend," Sadie said. "She's here somewhere." She remembered Ms. Petreli urging them to stick to the buddy system until the killer was caught, lest someone else end up like Katie Philips. "I should get back to her actually." *Better make sure Olivia's safe.*

Dante frowned with disappointment. Sadie didn't mind since he'd ditched her first the night before.

"Hopefully I'll see you around," Dante said. He pulled out a pre-rolled joint from his pocket and lit it.

"Maybe you will," Sadie said, resisting the urge to stay back to smoke with him. "Who knows, you might get lucky."

Dante's eyes brightened at that, and Sadie turned back to the house, pleased with herself. Messing with guys was almost *too* easy.

Sadie retraced her steps back through the house, scared she'd get lost otherwise, which brought her back to the pool room and face-to-face with Claire Gostosi. She was still half-naked and wet in her bikini, and as usual, she did not look happy to see Sadie.

Next to her was Bree, Claire's puppet and Olivia's man-stealer. Sadie made a side-step to get around them, but Claire blocked her path.

What a brave little idiot.

"What are *you* doing here?" Claire slurred. She was drunk, her eyes unable to focus and not quite steady on her feet.

Sadie was so tired of this. She had been Claire's target ever since her first day at Bellewood Prep, when she refused to conform to Claire's idea of how she should look and behave. She didn't *have* to put up with this treatment. She refused to do so now. "I was invited."

"As if. Who would invite a freak like *you?*"

Bree chuckled at Claire's less than clever quip.

"I guess it doesn't matter, because here I am." Sadie attempted a second time to step around her. Once again, Claire blocked her.

If only Claire knew what Sadie was capable of. She'd be shocked to know what happened to that girl at her old school; Sadie's expulsion after the fact was a small price to pay for the satisfaction of exacting revenge. Claire, for all her idiocy, was fairly harmless. She'd whisper stupid insults, spread outrageous rumors, but was usually non-violent. She appeared now, however, to be just drunk enough to do something stupid, and Sadie struggled to handle her reactions.

"This is what's going to happen," Sadie warned, a fire in her glare. "I'm going to give you till the count of three to get out of my way, because I need to find my friend."

Sadie waited a moment, but Claire made no move to leave. Instead, her drunk face contorted into a grimace, as if outraged that Sadie would presume to tell her what to do.

"Three.... Two...."

Before she got to one, Claire's drink was airborne, swung from her glass into Sadie's face, soaking her.

Sadie's face morphed to a malicious grin. Now there'd be hell to pay.

"You shouldn't have done that."

CHAPTER SEVEN

"What did you say, bitch?" Claire demanded, emboldened by her perceived victory, even as Bree backed away, distancing herself from her.

Sadie matched her stare, unmoved by whatever ferocity Claire was trying to conjure. She went too far. It's not like Sadie hadn't warned her. With a trembling hand, she wiped some of the drink still dripping off her face.

"I said you shouldn't have done that." Her voice was steel, and her onyx eyes took on an ominous glow. Every nerve in her body sparked with electricity; her heart beat with the same intensity as a stampede. *This time she will learn her lesson.*

Claire, too drunk and stupid to back down, grabbed for the closest weapon she could find, the beer bottle in Bree's hand, swung and smashed it against Sadie's head.

Sadie lunged forward and the girls tumbled to the ground, rolling around as a crowd converged on them. Sadie saw her opportunity and lashed out, striking hard.

Claire howled in pain and held both hands to her face. Sadie released her.

"Stop this!" Destiny Yu emerged from the crowd and took Sadie by the arm, separating her from Claire.

"Look at what this bitch did to me!" Claire shrieked. A scarlet, diagonal line had formed from her right ear to the left side of her chin, dripping blood onto the marble floor.

Sadie would have been happy to pounce again, but Destiny had placed herself between them.

"*She attacked me!*" Claire screamed louder this time. "I'm bleeding!"

Destiny surveyed the area. "There's broken glass everywhere, you must have gotten cut when you were rolling around on the floor."

Destiny put a protective hand on Sadie's shoulder, led her away from the chaos. "Are you okay?" she asked when they were away from the crowd.

"She got me in the head with a bottle," Sadie said. She forced a calming breath and gradually she relaxed, but her trembling hands betrayed her disbelief. She'd underestimated Claire's stupidity.

"Hey, at least you won," Destiny said with a wicked grin spread on her lips.

Sadie couldn't help but laugh. She *had* won, and now Claire's lesson was learned.

"I think the party's over," Destiny said as she pulled some stray pieces of glass out of Sadie's hair. "Let's get out of here?"

Sadie was glad to have Destiny's support, she was sure if Olivia had witnessed the fight, she would have had the opposite reaction. Maybe Destiny wasn't so bad. Sadie nodded and followed Destiny.

As they walked out, Sadie looked back at Claire, still sobbing and clutching her face.

For a moment, Sadie brimmed with pride.

CHAPTER EIGHT

"It looks fine. Great, actually." Destiny was inspecting Sadie's head injury, but found no wound.

Sadie remained silent. How could she explain that she healed at preternatural speed, when she herself didn't understand it?

They were a block away from Brock's mansion, standing outside Destiny's old, purple Subaru. While most Bellewood basics drove around in high-end luxury vehicles, here was Destiny, proud of her beater. Sadie decided it added to her charm.

"Thanks for getting me out of there," Sadie said to her new friend. "It could have ended badly."

"I don't doubt that." Destiny eyed Sadie intensely, trying to understand her.

It made her uncomfortable, but Sadie knew Destiny wouldn't get very far. Her maze of secrets was closely held and never discovered.

The music coming from Brock's house was back in full blast. Sadie guessed Claire was finished with her moment.

"Looks like the party's still going after all," Sadie said, though she was glad to be out of there.

"Well just because we aren't there, doesn't mean the party has to end for us."

Sadie was unsure what Destiny meant, and she was too afraid to ask. She couldn't help but wonder what Olivia would think about her hanging out with Destiny, but quickly shook the thought from her mind. As far as she knew, Olivia was still at the party enjoying herself, and wasn't here to stop her.

Destiny's face changed, a conspirator to some unknown plan. Her eyes gleamed. "Let's go make some money."

#

Destiny's Subaru was eccentric; old, but modified and maintained to perfection. Its engine roared with every acceleration, revealing a powerful, modern piece of machinery under the hood. A pair of fuzzy dice dangled from the rearview, spent joints littered the cup-holders in the center console, and the back seat had been removed and replaced with a luscious mattress, pillows, and blankets.

Destiny's taste in music was equally eccentric. Each song she select- ed was different from the next. From techno, to heavy metal, then pop, each song boomed from the car's expensive speakers.

"*Way back playback!*" Destiny exclaimed as a song from their child- hood came on.

Sadie couldn't help but match her enthusiasm. *Such a good song.* They sang out loud together, off-key and adding their own lyrics when they forgot the words, until their bellies ached from laughter.

Destiny proved to be a complete surprise to Sadie in the best way possible. Olivia had nothing positive to say about her back at the party, but Sadie was having the *best* time with Destiny. She was wild and carefree and it was contagious.

They were forty minutes outside of town now, driving through the main road in the Coquette Woods, until Destiny made a sharp turn. The wheels spun on dirt road for a second, and the vehicle vibrated as the car sped across uneven terrain.

"Nervous?" Destiny asked, taking note of the shift in energy.

"Please," Sadie scoffed. "I just wish you would have told me we were taking a hike; I would have worn better clothes." She motioned to her too-short dress and too-high heels.

Destiny laughed. "That might come in handy where we're going."

"What do you mean?" Sadie asked, trying her best to sound cool.

"You'll see."

Soon, Destiny made another turn onto another dirt path. They were well off the beaten track now. Ahead, a large, fenced compound came into view. They followed the path that led to an opening in the fencing, flanked on both sides by what looked like watchtowers. Sadie wondered if there were people inside, watching them approach. Beyond the towers was a large, steel building shaped like a barn. A yellow glow shone through the tiny windows that decorated the exterior, and voices sounded from inside. Even from this distance, Sadie could make it out to be three men.

Destiny parked the car, and Sadie, now on high alert, followed her to the building's entrance. The sound of their shoes crunching on gravel echoed in the wind, and despite the muffled chatter inside the building, there was an eerie quiet. She asked herself what Olivia would do. *She definitely wouldn't agree to accompany Destiny, of all people, to a sketchy-ass warehouse in the middle of nowhere. Okay, next obvious solution: Get the hell out of here.*

"Destiny, I–"

Sadie was interrupted by the sudden pounding of Destiny's fist against the steel door.

"Password?" a grizzled voice shouted from inside.

"Apple," Destiny replied.

"The computer or the fruit?" the man on the other side spat.

Destiny rolled her eyes. "Fruit."

Sadie's heart raced. Destiny made a mistake bringing them here, she was certain they were in serious danger. Her mind worked to assess how high she would have to jump to scale the fence laterally, to avoid the obvious guards stationed in the watchtower, and wondered if she could carry Destiny in the process too.

Two loud CLICKS sounded from the doors, and Sadie held her breath and braced herself as the door creaked open.

A tall, scrawny man met them on the other side, his wrinkled face twisted mean, with a rifle in his hands aimed at Sadie's head.

Fuck.

CHAPTER NINE

Sadie was ready to go on the offensive as another man calmly emerged and patted Destiny down. Destiny raised her arms to the side as the man did his search, seemingly unphased by it all.

"What....*the hell*?" Sadie stammered at the man still pointing a gun in her face.

"It's cool," Destiny told her, as though that would be reassuring.

The man that was patting Destiny down moved over to Sadie, rubbing his hands up and down her body. She didn't imagine it when his hands lingered a little too long on her backside. She fantasized about how she would kill him after taking care of the man with the gun.

"They're good," the one patting her down muttered to the man with the rifle, signaling him to lower the weapon. He proceeded to shake Destiny's hand, and ushered them inside. He looked as if he hadn't slept or eaten in days and Sadie was sure as hell not about to let him cannibalize her.

Destiny took Sadie's hand and urged her on. When it was clear Destiny intended to follow the scary men into the warehouse, Sadie decided she had to follow, if only to protect her.

Most of the interior of the warehouse was bare save for a few stray couches and chairs, where two men sat with beers, locked in conversation. Three long, steel tables marked the centerpiece of the space where another man sat wrapping thick rectangular packages with cellophane. It didn't require much of an imagination to guess what was inside, and Sadie started to question her decision in entertaining Destiny's offer to work with her. A few more men were scattered about the building. Some were clicking away aggressively on game consoles and taking bong hits in another makeshift living area. Others stood about talking, cigarettes and beer in hand. With every step Sadie took, her high heels echoed against the steel walls, and some of the men stopped to stare and catcall. She pulled her dress down lower, cursing Olivia for the tenth time that night for choosing her outfit.

They were taken to an office at the back of the building, and the man nodded to them before stalking away. Destiny opened the door, and another man in his thirties sat behind a desk, with his feet propped on top. He had olive skin, and his jet black hair was slicked back. His arms were positioned behind his head like an imaginary pillow, as if he was sitting in a hammock on the beach rather than a creaky armchair in an abandoned warehouse. Sadie could tell from his clean shaven face to his gold chains, all the way down to his snake-skin shoes, that he was the boss of this operation. His eyes traveled up and down their bodies, taking in their figures. Destiny remained stone faced, obviously used to this routine. Sadie could feel bile rising in her throat, and wasn't sure if it was from his obscene gesture or his cheap taste in cologne.

"You brought a friend, Destiny. Is her name Fate?" He laughed at his own joke.

"This is Sadie. I want her to help," Destiny replied. To Sadie, she said, "this is–well, we *call him* Jefe."

He took another long look at Sadie, drinking her in. Sadie had had the longest day, her hair was sticky and matted from the beer that Claire had tossed on her, and her feet ached terribly. Tiny dress or not, she was sure she looked like hell. Either *Jefe* had low standards, or Sadie looked better than she thought.

Sadie matched his gaze intensely, hoping he could read the *fuck you* she was thinking at him in her eyes. It seemed to work. Within moments, he tore his eyes away and cleared his throat, visibly uncomfortable. *That's better.*

"New shipment of *Bliss* just came in," Jefe said. "The formula's been tweaked a bit. Produces even more intense hallucinations and euphoria. The kids are gonna love it, and we'll all stand to make a fair bit of money from this."

Bliss. The drug that was all over the news, according to Olivia.

"Does the new formula make it safer?" Sadie asked, recalling what Olivia had told her about a spurt of overdoses.

"How should I know, kid? I just sell the stuff."

"I'll take all of it," Destiny said.

\#

Destiny drove to town far slower than she had on their way to the warehouse. Sadie guessed a car full of drugs was a good enough reason to obey the speed limit.

"How many times have you done this?"

Destiny giggled. "Enough to know that everything is going to be okay. You don't have to worry."

But Sadie *was* worried. She knew what Destiny was all about, Olivia had even warned her, but somehow she still allowed herself to be pulled into this situation. Apart from the odd joint, Sadie had never done drugs before, and now she was traveling in a car full of it.

But it wasn't herself she was worried about. Her mind wandered to Olivia, her dearest friend. How would she take it if she knew what Sadie was up to?

And Destiny? Sadie worried about her too. If she was found out, there would be real consequences to pay.

Sadie didn't need to worry about herself. Not really. If the police pulled them over now, she knew she could outrun any officer. But even if they did manage to arrest her and lock her up, there was no jail cell that could hold her for long. In this way, Sadie's curse was also her gift.

"The thing about selling drugs, Sadie, is that you want to move them as fast as possible. Luckily, I have a *great* customer. Let's make one more stop tonight before I take you home, so we can get rid of this product, and then I'll have my bed back."

Sadie glanced at the back seat that was also a mattress, where all the Bliss was piled.

"Bed?"

Destiny's expression turned somber. "Do you think I'd be selling drugs if I had some fancy mansion to go home to?" After a moment, she elaborated. "I'm not homeless or anything. I just don't get along with my stepdad. It's easier if I spend most nights in my car."

They drove the rest of the way in silence. Sadie didn't have a great family life either, but at least she had a real bed and home to go back to and live in peace. She imagined that if she didn't, the decision to sell drugs would be easy to make.

Her phone buzzed. It was a message from Olivia. Sadie assumed her friend was asking where she'd gone and who she left with, but it was hard to tell through the drunken typos.

"Is that your boyfriend?" Destiny asked. She tried to sound nonchalant, but Sadie wondered what the real meaning behind the question was.

"I'm single," Sadie said, "I thought that much was obvious."

"I'm glad to hear it," Destiny replied. After a moment, she put her hand on Sadie's leg.

Sadie reddened, but Destiny's eyes were on the road so she couldn't see it.

She could have easily moved Destiny's hand. But maybe she liked how it felt there.

Sadie ignored the text, but swore to herself the next time Olivia had something negative to say about Destiny, Sadie would defend her.

CHAPTER TEN

It was already past 2:00 am when they made it back to town from the Coquette Woods. Sadie was glad school was canceled, but felt guilty that a girl had to die so she could sleep in.

They drove along the Bellewood Shore, the moonlight reflected off the waters casting the only light around them.

Destiny's hand was still in Sadie's lap, but she didn't mind. In time, Sadie's hand found Destiny's, and though they barely knew each other, holding hands felt like the most natural thing in the world.

"I think I could get used to this," Destiny told her.

It was an intriguing thought, one Sadie had never explored before. She stayed silent to save herself the embarrassment of what she might have said. *I've never done this with a girl.* Too childish. *I don't let anyone get too close to me.* Too dark.

Sadie was surprised when Destiny pulled the car over. What was about to happen next? Holding hands she could handle, but anything more...

"We're here," Destiny said. She turned the engine off and stepped out.

They were right outside the abandoned waterfront amusement park. It seemed like an odd place to meet someone, but after the night Sadie had, nothing could surprise her. She exited the vehicle and watched as Destiny collected the Bliss from the top of the mattress in the back seat.

Now that she was paying closer attention, Sadie could see that Destiny also had a duffel bag stuffed behind the front seats, and various clothing items strewn throughout. Evidence of just how much time Destiny spent in this car. Sadie's heart sank further.

"Help me with these." Destiny handed Sadie a few bags of the Bliss.

Now that it was in her hand, Sadie noticed the Bliss came in pill form. Tiny tablets with miniature hearts etched on them, making them look like candy. Whoever was responsible for the Bliss tablets had a knack for marketing.

Destiny took the rest of the Bliss from the car, and led the way to the gates of the park.

As always, the haunting statue of the lady in the flowing dress stood guard outside the rusted gates. Sadie could see a warning in her stone eyes. *Stay away,* it seemed to say, but Sadie wasn't sure what to stay away from—from the park, or Destiny.

"Need help getting over the fence?" Destiny asked.

Sadie stifled the urge to laugh. The gate stood eight feet tall, Sadie could easily scale it in a casual hop. Instead, she grabbed hold of the gate and made it seem as if her feet struggled to find purchase, and slowly, but easily, climbed the fence landing nimbly on the other side.

Destiny's expression betrayed how impressed she was. She passed the pills she was holding to Sadie through the opening of the gate, and climbed it to the other side. She was only slightly out of breath at the end of it.

"Looks like you've jumped this fence before?"

"Once or twice," Sadie lied. She'd never been in this park, but it was easier to let Destiny think she had. The less questions she asked about who Sadie was and what she could do, the better.

They walked the park together, and when Destiny reached for Sadie's hand, she let her hold it. It was nice, this closeness. Sadie was used to being alone, but she'd never been as alone as she had been in the last several months. Since the last time she saw her father.

While it was true that she had a friend in Olivia, Sadie always had to censor herself around her. To show her true self to anyone, let alone her only friend, would be catastrophic. But being here with Destiny, it felt as though for once she wouldn't be judged. Destiny had her own secrets and her own hard history. Sadie had the sense that there was so much more to Destiny behind her cool facade.

They passed the many abandoned concession stands and various rides, rusted with neglect. The waterslides overlooking the ocean in the park's rear, the trick mirror playground, and the carousel where they were sitting now, all added to the mystique of the evening.

Destiny reached out to tuck Sadie's hair behind her ear. "Your hair is always hiding your face, did you know that?"

They sat only inches apart, and Destiny looked at Sadie as if seeing her, *really* seeing her—all the parts that no one could ever know. Sadie shifted under Destiny's intense gaze, nervous and unsure how far this would go.

"You have the most beautiful lips," Destiny whispered, and then she was leaning into her.

Sadie's heart skipped a beat. This was it. Her first kiss with another woman. She closed her eyes. Leaned in too. And then a sound in the distance stopped them before their lips met.

There was someone else in the park—a man, Sadie sensed—walking toward them.

Sadie gasped as if looking at a ghost. It was Dante Nerosi.

"Here he is," Destiny said loud enough so that Dante could hear her. "My number one customer!"

CHAPTER ELEVEN

Dante is Destiny's best customer? He's the one that's going to be buying all this Bliss?

Sadie now realized Oliva was not exaggerating when she was talking about just how prevalent the 'drug problem' was.

When Dante reached them at the carousel, Destiny stood and jumped on him, playfully planting a kiss on his cheek.

"How's it going stud?" she asked, swinging from his hip.

"I'm hanging out at a haunted park in the middle of the night, so never better. Who did you bring with you?" He looked at Sadie for the first time since he reached them, and the realization struck him. "It's you," he said, surprised at seeing her.

"It's me," Sadie echoed. She stood to greet him. A part of her wanted to jump up on him too, as Destiny had, but she didn't want to scare him off. She leaned in for a quick hug instead. She hoped he didn't notice, but she breathed in his scent, deep and slow; it was even more intoxicating than before. When she pulled back, his face was close to hers, as close as Destiny's had been moments ago, and his brilliant green eyes shone under the full moon above them.

"You guys know each other?" Destiny asked.

Awkward. Destiny didn't seem like the jealous type, but they were just about to kiss before Dante had walked up on them. And though Destiny couldn't know this, now that Dante was here, Sadie could only think about him.

Destiny filled Dante in about the new batch of Bliss they'd just picked up, though she left out any real details. Sadie got the sense that Destiny's connections were private, so she made a mental note to not bring up the warehouse in the middle of nowhere or the gun that had been pointed at her face.

All while Destiny was talking, Sadie was staring at Dante, drinking in every detail. More than once when he glanced at her, his eyes moved up and down over her whole body. For the first time all night, Sadie was grateful for the tiny dress she was wearing, and when it rose slightly when she moved, she didn't pull it down.

Destiny might have noticed Dante staring, because she moved closer to Sadie, as if protectively. Sadie felt the weight of Destiny's closeness, and it was uncomfortable in Dante's presence.

"So how much do you want?" Destiny asked him.

"Do you really have to ask?"

Dante handed her the biggest wad of cash Sadie had ever seen, after which Destiny, looking pleased, handed him all the bags of Bliss.

"Is that all for yourself?" Sadie asked, unable to help herself. It was far too much for one person to possibly ever take.

Dante laughed. "Definitely not. I hardly touch the shit. But when the allowance runs out, having these money makers around helps."

"Oh? Daddy doesn't give you enough?" Destiny said this teasingly, but Sadie could hear the bitterness in her tone.

"The money comes from my grandma, actually," Dante said, not noting the sarcasm. Sadie presumed he might not know that Destiny's situation wasn't like most Bellewood kids'. Or her own, for that matter. "But she wants me to be responsible, so she limits my access to the trust fund. It's a good thing I got you to help make ends meet, Destiny."

"You don't have a clue what 'making ends meet' means, but that's okay. Live your best life, boo. Sadie and I are going to head out now."

Sadie deflated. She was excited to be near Dante again, she wasn't ready for it to be over.

"So soon?" Dante asked. He sounded hurt, as if he was being left out of the party.

"It's *late*," Destiny exclaimed. "Plus, I think my girl here has had enough excitement for one night."

That might have been true, but with Dante here now, Sadie was open to some more excitement.

"So what if it's late?" Dante protested. "Not like you gotta get up early, right? I heard the news. School's canceled till further notice because of what happened to that girl..." His gaze shot down. Sadie could tell the details of how Katie was murdered made him uncomfortable.

"There are some *sick* fucks out there, that's for sure," Destiny said with a shudder.

"So you guys aren't going to leave me out here alone, are you? Especially after what they said on the news? They said to travel in pairs, that it wasn't safe to be alone."

He looked at Sadie as if imploring her for company. She smiled, willing to comply. It was Destiny that had to be convinced.

"You said this batch has a new formula?" Dante asked Destiny, motioning to the bags in his hand. "It's supposed to give you a better high?"

"That's what we were told." Destiny shrugged, but Sadie could tell what Dante was getting at.

"Well, why don't we try them out and see for ourselves?"

CHAPTER TWELVE

Sadie's heart pounded with anticipation. A part of her didn't want to go through with it, but a larger part, the part that won, was content to sit back and see what would happen.

Dante sat opposite their carriage on the carousel, and he was the first to swallow Bliss. Nobody had any liquids on them, so he dry-swallowed the drug with an ease that suggested he'd done this before.

"Now we wait," he said with a smirk. His eyes twinkled with excitement, and despite the insidiousness of it all, Sadie thought he looked utterly adorable. Like a little boy, ecstatic about playtime.

He handed a single pill to Destiny, but she looked at Sadie and hesitated. "Are you sure about this? I can drive you home if you've changed your mind."

"What the hell?" Dante protested. "I just dropped! You can't let me trip alone!"

"*Can,* and will," Destiny retorted. "If Sadie doesn't want to do it."

Dante looked at Sadie, expectant, but his demeanor revealed he already knew her answer.

"I want to try." Sadie tried to hide the shakiness in her voice. "Let's do it." She thought of Olivia then, but pushed her out of her mind.

Destiny dry-swallowed her own pill and then reached for another Dante's bag.

"One hit is all it takes," she whispered, reaching over to Sadie and placing it onto her tongue herself. Her face was only inches away from Sadie's when she opened her mouth to show her she had swallowed the pill.

"I see you ladies are getting better acquainted," Dante mused, a sly smile forming across his lips.

I'd like to get better acquainted with you, Sadie thought. She reminded herself to keep her wits about her, lest she slip up and say something embarrassing in front of him. Again.

"I wish we were getting acquainted faster," Destiny said with a wink before sitting back, giving Sadie some space.

The next several minutes passed in idle chatter, story telling, joke making, things normal teens might do together; things Sadie might have experienced already if she was normal.

After some time Sadie settled into a comfort she'd never felt before, though she doubted she was high. Dante and Destiny seemed just fine, as did she, save for a greater sense of tranquility.

They exchanged stories, one by one. Sadie learned that most of Dante's friends had left Bellewood for universities in bigger cities. She got the sense he was lost and lonely, chasing good times so he wouldn't feel so alone.

Destiny had shared her plans for the future. She loved Bellewood but hated her family. She was ready to leave it all behind to start anew.

It was the reason she worked so much. She was saving her money to one day leave and never look back.

While Sadie was nothing if not secretive, she found she was sharing stories of her own, but was careful to stop herself before revealing too much information. Instead, she talked about living alone, and that before Bellewood she'd lived with her father. She didn't mention what became of him. She talked about the house in the woods she'd lived in as a little girl with her father and her mother. She wouldn't even let herself think of what became of *her*. When they asked her probing questions, she'd answer more freely than she normally would have, but she was already so practiced at delivering her boxed, surface answers, that anything she said was hardly sincere.

After some time, they decided to explore the park, and upon standing, Sadie admitted she might have been starting to feel it.

Dante placed his arm around her, laughing. "Just wait until it really hits, you're gonna love it."

"Spoken like a true junkie," Destiny teased. She was walking a few feet ahead of them, and Sadie noted that it was the farthest apart they'd been since she rescued her from kicking Claire's ass.

"I'm just partying!" Dante protested, a bit too loud, like Destiny's words had stung. "And is that really the way you want to speak to your number one customer?"

Destiny ignored him.

Sadie wasn't sure if it was the drugs making her paranoid, but she could feel tension between Dante and Destiny.

By the time they came upon the Ferris wheel, the same one Sadie could see from her balcony, the high had taken full effect. Though there was no electricity running through the park, it appeared to be lit up, and Sadie imagined the ride in its prime over a hundred years ago—all the young people that would have enjoyed it. All dead and gone.

Dante stepped onto the platform where the nearest seats were, unlatched the safety belt, then beckoned to Sadie to sit. Things were starting to spin, so Sadie welcomed the seat.

Dante sat next to her. There wasn't space for anyone else, so Destiny, excluded, just stood by. Sadie felt guilty; she thought she should at least offer Destiny her own seat, and she could stand. But Dante was so close to her now, and it was nice to have him pressed against her.

"I wonder if this has an on-switch," Destiny said, searching.

"It better not," Sadie said, wide-eyed. Taking rides in amusement parks was not part of her upbringing, and she didn't want to start now on a hundred-year-old machine.

"Relax girlie, I'll catch you." Destiny gave one of her playful winks again.

Dante's arm wrapped around Sadie, giving her shoulder a squeeze. "Don't worry, I won't let you fall."

Destiny glared at them before turning away. Maybe there *was* some jealousy there. Sadie hid a smile.

Widening his arms, Dante said, "Squeeze in Destiny, there's plenty of Dante to go around."

Sadie wasn't used to sharing, but if it meant a chance with Dante, then she just might be willing to.

"I'll pass, you lovers enjoy yourselves."

Sadie braced herself, but Dante didn't react at all to Destiny's quip. And being seated next to him, the rush of the drug flowing through her, and the warmth of his arm around her, Sadie could almost imagine they actually were lovers.

"Waste the buzz if you guys want," Destiny said, sounding bored, if not hurt, "but I'm going to go explore. Everything is so shiny right now, I don't want to miss a thing."

Sadie watched her walk away and imagined she was annoyed. She was too high to do anything about it, though. Everything *was* shiny, and Sadie just wanted to enjoy it. The fact that Dante was pressed against her, enjoying it too, was an added bonus.

Once Destiny was out of view, Dante whispered, "I'm glad you're out here, don't get me wrong, but what are you doing hanging out with Destiny Yu?"

"What? I like her," Sadie said, her words dreamlike and lofty. She didn't whisper because she was sure Destiny was out of earshot now, and there was no one Sadie knew who had as sharp hearing as her own.

"Well she definitely likes *you* too, that's for sure. Did you see how she was looking at me like she wanted to kill me? She's totally pissed that we're hitting it off."

We're hitting it off? Sadie was thrilled.

"Just be careful around her," Dante continued. "There's always been something about that girl I don't trust."

Sadie realized it was the second time that night she was being warned about Destiny. First Olivia, now Dante. She could have asked what exactly about Destiny made her untrustworthy, but Dante was already leaning in, his breath coming in short, fast waves.

And then his lips were pressed against hers.

He tasted of cigarettes and liquor, and Sadie wanted more. Her lips parted and his tongue found hers. Dante kissed her gently at first, then more intensely as Sadie gave into the moment. She wanted him so badly, and he wanted her too.

She didn't stop him when his hands searched her body, and he moaned when she felt him. When he stood, she followed, and when he took off his shirt, she took off her dress and spread it out on the platform to lay on it like a blanket.

And then he was on her, kissing her harder. Her nails ran along his smooth back, and when she decided it was her turn to get on top, he gasped at the force she used to pin him down.

And there in the open, at the foot of an ancient ferris wheel under the glow of a full moon, when their desperation for each other grew and the kissing wasn't enough, they did more.

CHAPTER THIRTEEN

It was midday the next morning by the time Sadie woke. A dull headache lingered in the center of her forehead, and she found she was *too* thirsty—her insides dry and aching—so she forced herself out of bed, and stumbled to the kitchen sink. She guzzled water straight from the tap, and then stumbled back into bed, naked as the day she was born.

Only after getting back to bed and seeing what she assumed to be mud on her skin and bedsheets did she realize she didn't remember getting there.

She'd taken Bliss with Destiny and Dante, of that she was sure. She'd also had some wine to drink earlier in the night, before arriving at Brock's party, which doubtlessly contributed to her foggy memory.

Sadie racked her mind, trying to recall the night before.

She remembered taking Bliss. She remembered the Ferris wheel, and Destiny storming off. Danté's passionate hands over her, his hard body under hers... And then nothing

Why can't I remember arriving home? Why am I covered in mud?

The only thing she did know was that she was *never* taking Bliss again.

Her phone buzzed on her bedside table, and Sadie was thankful she hadn't lost it in her drug-induced fog. She reached for her phone, expecting it to be Olivia checking in, but it was Destiny who'd messaged: *I've got a killer migraine. Did you get home ok?*

Sadie messaged that she was home but didn't remember getting there.

I hope you didn't walk, Destiny answered, *but I was way too out of it to drive. Besides, it seemed like you wanted to be alone with Dante anyway.*

Sadie *had* wanted to be alone with Dante, but she wasn't about to say that to the girl who was obviously interested in her. Instead, she messaged back, *where did you go after you walked off?*

Back to my car. Things started spinning so I slept it off.

Memories of the park spinning around her came back to her too, and the thought made her nauseous.

Her phone buzzed again: *I'd like to see you again today? Unless you're too busy with Dante.*

Sadie ignored that message. She knew things could get... awkward with Destiny again, and after the night she'd spent with Dante, she wanted to see where that would go.

She searched her phone and was ashamed she didn't save his number when she had the chance. Hungover or not, she'd love to be spending the day with *him*, and Destiny would just have to understand that. Sadie searched for him online, and found his picture and name attached to a private profile that she was sure belonged to him.

She sent Dante a follow request, and doom scrolled her phone, anxious for his reply.

An hour passed until her phone buzzed again, and her heart leapt hoping it was Dante. She was a bit disappointed to see it was Olivia getting in touch, but when she read her message her heart raced again.

Can you meet me at the hospital ASAP? It's URGENT!

CHAPTER FOURTEEN

Sadie was damp with sweat when she burst through the hospital doors twenty minutes later. St. John's was on the other side of town, but it was a quiet day in Bellewood, and when nobody was around to see it, she allowed herself to run at full speed, passing great distances easily.

She was in the emergency room and didn't know what to do next. Shaking, she worried if Olivia was okay. Rushing to the nurse's station, eyes welling with panicked tears, she was about to ask the triage nurse where to find her friend.

"Sadie! Thank you so much for coming." Olivia burst through the doors, wrapping Sadie in a desperate embrace. She let go a moment later, frowning. "You're wet."

"I got here as fast as I could," Sadie said. She was relieved, albeit confused, to see her best friend up and moving. On the run over she'd been imagining the worst. "You're all right?"

"Shaken, is all. I'm sorry I scared you. But I needed my best friend."

Sadie's heart warmed. She didn't realize just how much she needed Olivia too, until she was worried something bad had happened to her.

"It's Mitchell," Olivia said, tears clouding her eyes. "It's not good, Sadie." She broke into sobs, and all Sadie could do was hug her. "It must have been when I was hanging out with Brock at his party, after you left."

"What happened?" Sadie demanded, her panic rising.

"Those *stupid* drugs," Olivia spat.

For a moment, Sadie was stunned.

"People must have been taking them at the party, but I had no idea," Olivia continued. "I am such an *ass!* I told myself I was going to the party to try to get to the bottom of it, and all I did was hook up with Brock!"

"Olivia! What happened?"

She was crying again. "Mitchell *overdosed* last night!"

CHAPTER FIFTEEN

"He was drinking, so he wasn't thinking clearly," Olivia reasoned. "It's *never* a good idea to mix drugs with alcohol, especially when you don't know what you're taking."

They were in the waiting room of the ICU, whispering in a corner as other people sobbed and whispered around them. Apparently it hadn't been the only overdose of the night.

"So he still hasn't woken up?" Sadie asked, a sadness twisting her stomach.

Olivia shook her head. "No one even knew he overdosed until early this morning... One of Brock's house cleaners found him in the billiard room. Alone and blue in the face from lack of oxygen."

Guilt overwhelmed Sadie. She knew Mitchell was drunk at the party, and instead of hanging out with him she chose to get into an altercation with Claire and leave early. Claire had been asking for it, but Sadie should have known better. *I should have been there.*

The grim realization that she herself had taken Bliss without knowing its effects dawned on her. And before that? She'd picked up a batch from a shady warehouse with Destiny with the intention to sell. It might not have been from the same batch, but if Mitchell had overdosed on Bliss, then Sadie had become part of the problem.

All these thoughts plagued her, but she couldn't share any of them with Olivia. Not if she wanted to keep her as a friend.

So they sat in silence, holding hands just to feel the life pulsing through each other's veins. Mitchell's parents were in the room with him now, and didn't want anybody else with them. Sadie understood, they almost lost their son. When she saw them come out of the room, she could tell they'd been crying.

As horrible as Mitchell's situation is, Sadie thought, *at least he has parents who love him*. It was far more than she'd had for a long time.

Olivia stood up, it looked as if she was about to approach Mitchell's parents, when an audible gasp filled the room.

From the other side of the waiting room, someone turned up the volume on the television that hung on the wall, the local news was on the screen.

The whole room was holding their breath as they took in the desperate, terrified words of the news anchor.

A grueling discovery this afternoon. Another young woman was found murdered along the Bellewood shore. Eye witnesses report the body appeared mutilated in the same way as Katie Phillips, the young woman who was tragically murdered only two nights ago. Like Katie, the young woman's face had been brutally disfigured, and a hole in the chest cavity revealed her heart had been removed, leading experts to believe the murders are most likely related. Residents are being urged to be on high alert, as who is being called 'The Heartbreak Killer' is still on the loose.

CHAPTER SIXTEEN

The room erupted in panic, some sharing nervous glances, others making desperate calls to their loved ones to check if they were safe. There was a murderer on the loose in Bellewood, targeting young women, and no one felt safe.

Olivia was still watching the news, wide-eyed and mouth agape, shocked at what was being reported. When she finally spoke, Sadie didn't like what she had to say. "We have to get down there."

"To the *crime scene*?"

"We have to do *something*," Olivia despaired.

"Liv, the experts are on it. Let them do their jobs."

"So we just sit around and do *nothing*? While this town goes to shit?"

"I know you're upset, Olivia. This is a *very* upsetting situation. But we don't have to go down there and put ourselves at risk."

"I swore to myself I'd get to the bottom of the drug problem in Bellewood," Olivia said, a determination in her voice. "But I did nothing, and Mitchell almost died."

Sadie knew where Olivia was going with this, and convincing her otherwise seemed like a losing battle.

"And now there's a *Heartbreak Killer* murdering young women. I *need* to help however I can. I'll go down to the scene of the crime alone if I have to."

\#

Olivia saying she was willing to go to the scene of a murder alone was all it took for a begrudging Sadie to accept going along with her, if only to keep her safe. There was a maniac on the loose, and Olivia was *not* going to be his next victim.

They drove along the shore in Olivia's BMW, eyes peeled for unusual activity. The news report wasn't clear where along the coast the woman's body was found, likely to keep people from storming the scene.

But Olivia was determined.

When they passed the scene of Katie Phillips' murder, Olivia slowed down. Except for a large vigil of flowers and candles, there was nothing out of the ordinary.

They continued along the shore, and were now driving along the outskirts of town when Sadie thought they might have missed the scene. But soon enough she could see it—before Olivia could—a cluster of police vehicles and news vans parked ahead of them.

When Olivia's eyes could finally see what Sadie was already observing, she whispered, "It must have happened here."

Sadie remained quiet as Olivia pulled over, but a chill ran up her spine as she took in her surroundings.

They were parked just outside the abandoned waterfront amusement park, where Sadie had been partying in the early hours of that
morning.

CHAPTER SEVENTEEN

Having parked and exited the vehicle, they scoped the scene. Olivia inched her way closer, and Sadie followed, reluctant, but determined to keep her friend safe. Police tape cordoned off the area, and there were police officers on patrol to ensure no one would get too close. Sadie was relieved that the scene was cut off in such a way she wasn't forced to see a dead body.

Olivia was angling for a way to get closer to the scene when she let out a gasp.

"What is it?" Sadie asked, alarmed.

"Can you read that police officer's name tag?"

There was a young officer a few yards from them, standing guard right off the road, blocking the path down to the shore.

Sadie could clearly see his name tag read, *O'Brien*, but wasn't sure she should admit that to Olivia. Her friend had no clue just how strong Sadie's senses were.

"I think it starts with an *O*," Sadie offered.

"O'Brien?" Olivia asked, squinting with her neck stretched outward to get a closer look.

"Could be? Yeah, I think so."

"*That's* the officer I spoke to on the phone the other day. He's the one I'm supposed to be meeting with tomorrow to do my report on the Bellewood drug crisis."

"Exciting stuff," Sadie managed, dryly.

"I should go introduce myself. Maybe he'll share some information."

Before Sadie could talk her out of it, Olivia was off and headed toward the officer, so Sadie followed.

"I'm sorry, Miss, this area of the shore is closed," the young officer said as they approached him. "There's plenty of beach in either direction from here for you girls to walk along. But I wouldn't recommend it."

"We just want to talk," Olivia said to the officer. Sadie bristled at '*we*', but remained quiet. "Officer O'Brien, is it? I think we may have spoken before. My name is Olivia Baltimore, we have a meeting planned to talk about the Bellewood drug crisis."

"Oh, that's right," Officer O'Brien said with some recognition. He seemed timid. He wasn't much older than them, a few years at most, and he was around their same height too. It made talking to him next to a major crime scene far less intimidating.

Olivia introduced Sadie next, and when he shook her hand, Sadie could tell he had less interest in her. His eyes shot right back to Olivia's, and Sadie knew her friend was going to use that to her advantage.

"What can you tell us, Officer?"

"Call me Chad." He smiled. "But I'm really not supposed to say anything."

"We can keep a secret," Olivia whispered, but Sadie was sure she would write about this for the paper the first chance she got.

The officer looked around to make sure his colleagues wouldn't overhear him. "Well, there's been"—he lowered his voice—"*another murder*." Another uniformed officer approached, and Chad cleared his throat. "You two should get home and stay inside where it's safe."

Waiting until the other officer's back got smaller and smaller against the shoreline, the three stood together in an awkward silence.

"We know that much," Olivia said, now nobody could hear them. "Who was it? What was the motive behind it? What leads do we have on who the killer is?"

"Slow down," Chad said, his palms upturned and sweat dripping from his hairline. "All that information will be made public at the appropriate time."

And then a girl emerged from the crime scene, beyond the police tape behind Chad. She was crying, hair disheveled, a single red scab along her face, ear to cheek. Claire Gostosi.

"It was Bree!" she screamed, sobbing with black mascara running down her cheeks. "The Heartbreak Killer murdered my best friend!"

CHAPTER EIGHTEEN

Sadie gaped at Claire. It was weird enough to see her sporting a scab on her face after their fight, but to hear her say that *Bree Huxley* had just been murdered? When only the night before she was in fine form at Brock's party? It was too surreal.

Olivia made to walk past Chad to join Claire, but the officer moved to stop her.

"Claire, are you sure?" Olivia questioned, speaking over Chad's shoulder. Her voice came out like a gasp, and her eyes were wide in disbelief. Sadie knew any animosity Olivia might have held toward Bree—for hooking up with Joaquin while they were together—had been replaced with genuine concern.

"Of course I'm sure, she was my *best friend*!"

Sadie didn't think it was right to mention how horribly Claire had always treated Bree, and didn't think that qualified as a best friend.

"And now she's down there butchered like Katie! It isn't fair!"

"You shouldn't have gone down there," the officer warned.

"And you should have *prevented* this!" Claire shrieked, stepping closer. "How many more of my friends are going to die before you do *something?*"

"Claire, it's not his fault," Olivia said, grabbing the other girl's hand and dragging her away from Officer O'Brien. Sadie kept her distance. She doubted Claire would want to be comforted by her.

"What can you tell us?" Olivia urged when they made some distance.

"I didn't hear from her after the party last night," Claire said, sobbing. "We talk every morning, every time I message her she replies within seconds, it doesn't matter the time of day."

Sadie rolled her eyes, but that sounded about right.

"When she didn't get back to me all day I knew something was wrong. And then I came here to the shore, and saw it. *Her.* Lying there, crumpled, a *hole* in her chest. And I knew it must have been the same guy who killed Katie."

"But why were you here?" Sadie asked. She tried to hold it back, but couldn't hide the suspicion from her voice. "The story *just* broke on the news. And we're way off the outskirts of tow-"

"What am *I* doing here?" Claire screamed. Where she'd been crying moments ago, she now had the look of pure anger and hatred. "What the hell are *you* doing here?"

"Claire, relax," Olivia cut in. "She didn't mean anything by-"

"Like hell, she didn't!" Claire spat. "Honestly, Olivia, you should be ashamed of yourself, hanging around someone like *her.* She's bad news. You don't even know, do you? Look what this freak did to my face!"

Sadie crossed her arms, stayed silent, though she wanted to say she'd gladly cut Claire again.

"What are you talking about?" Olivia said.

"I guess you missed what happened since you spent the whole party in Brock's room," Claire said. "But I'm surprised your *friend* hasn't told you what she did. This psycho attacked me out of nowhere!"

"*You* provoked *me*, Claire," Sadie said, defending herself.

"Sadie? Did you really do this to Claire's face?"

This was the first time in their friendship Olivia was seeing this side of Sadie. The side she'd tried to hide for so long. She took a step back and looked away, avoiding eye contact. She couldn't face the look of Olivia's disappointment.

"Sadie, I'm your friend, but you can't get physical with people you don't like."

"That's not all," Claire continued, emboldened by Olivia's support. "After she attacked me, after she *gashed* my face open, she left the party with Destiny Yu."

Olivia looked at Sadie as if seeking clarity, but Sadie didn't deny it. She wouldn't outright lie to her friend's face.

"I bet she didn't tell you that, either," Claire continued, speaking to Olivia as if Sadie wasn't there. "And who the hell knows what they did from there? One thing's for sure, they were up to nothing good. And *everybody* knows Destiny's the bitch bringing Bliss into Bellewood."

Olivia looked as if she'd been struck. Sadie knew she'd let her down. She'd known how distrustful Olivia was of Destiny, but Sadie went off with her anyway. And Mitchell was lying in the hospital, comatose, because of Bliss.

"But there's more," Claire said, crying again. "They found drugs around Bree's body. Somehow, Bliss was involved in her murder."

CHAPTER NINETEEN

Claire's words resounded in Sadie's mind. *Bliss* had been found at the crime scene where Bree was murdered? Only a stone's throw away from the amusement park where she'd been with Destiny and Dante and a lot of Bliss changed hands? What the hell was going on?

"I knew it!" Olivia said. "I knew the drugs coming into Bellewood had to be part of the problem... But Sadie? You were hanging out with Destiny last night? After I *told* you what she was about? Why would you do that?"

"You were... with Brock," Sadie stammered, though she knew it was a poor excuse. She hadn't anticipated having this conversation. Not so soon anyway. "And after we fought," she said, referring to Claire, "Destiny was the only one who stood by me. She got me out of that situation, otherwise things could have ended way worse." She glared at Claire.

"Try it!" Claire said, balling her hands into fists and stepping closer to Sadie. "Go ahead, there's cops everywhere around here, get arrested. I want you to."

"Both of you, stop it!" Olivia demanded.

"After what she did to my face? Like hell am I going to drop it."

"Maybe next time you'll think twice before hitting me over the head with a bottle!"

"Stop it," Olivia screamed, and it was enough to get Officer Chad O'Brien's attention.

He walked over, shaking his head, and wiping at neck sweat. "Everything good over here?"

Claire looked as if she was about to spill all her problems onto him, but Olivia spoke first.

"We're fine, Officer—Chad."

He smirked, his eyes never wavering from Olivia's.

"It's been a very emotional few days," Olivia continued. "We're just all very upset."

"I understand that," he said, "but we've got police work to do here." After staring into her eyes for a few more moments, he then turned to Claire and said, "I'm very sorry you had to find your friend like this. Nobody deserves that. Just try to hang tight for a few more minutes, then we'll take you back to the station for some quick questions."

"What? Like I'm a suspect for my best friend's murder?"

"We're just trying to get to the bottom of this, Miss." He turned back to Olivia, smiled and said, "I really do think it's best for you to go home now. But we'll talk soon. I still owe you that interview." He shook her hand and walked off.

"Olivia, I—" Sadie started, but what could she say after having disappointed her friend so badly?

"Sadie, I think you should just go home."

"Olivia, please. I don't want to leave you like this."

"She told you to *leave*," Claire barked.

"Sadie, you know what getting to the bottom of the Bellewood drug crisis means to me. You knew I was suspicious of Destiny. And when Katie was murdered, I told you I suspected these awful drugs might somehow be involved. And still you left the party without telling me, to go hang out with *her*? I'm supposed to be your best friend, Sadie! What else is there that you're not telling me?"

If there was any point in time that Sadie was going to admit that not only was she with Destiny the previous night, but that she'd also spent it at the amusement park just a stone's throw away with bags full of Bliss, it might have been now. But she knew this was one more secret she would have to carry with her forever.

"Claire needs me, Sadie," Olivia said, as Claire clung to her desperately. And even though her *best friend* had just died, Sadie could see the smug look on Claire's face for having separated Sadie from her own best friend.

And when there was nothing else to do, because Olivia wouldn't even look at her, Sadie walked away, alone, back to her apartment.

A torrent of thoughts raged through her mind. Mitchell was in intensive care because of Bliss. Bree was murdered and Bliss was involved. Destiny was bringing Bliss into Bellewood. Dante was Destiny's best customer.

What have I gotten myself into?

Have I lost Olivia forever?

CHAPTER TWENTY

One sleepless night turned into three full days without rest.

Three days since Bree Huxley was killed, three days of self imposed lockdown at home, and three days without talking to her best friend.

This had been the longest she'd gone without talking to Olivia since they'd met in the fall. At first, Sadie thought some distance would be a good thing. A few days for Olivia to calm down, and then she'd reach out to her when she was ready to talk. But when Sadie picked up her phone for the millionth time, Olivia had still not reached out to her. If she was braver, she might have made the first call. But if Olivia rejected her? That was a pain she didn't want to face.

She had a missed call from Destiny. That was no surprise. Destiny had called at least once each night since the last time she'd seen her. But Sadie couldn't talk to her yet. For her own sake, and Destiny's. What if she freaked out on her? Was Destiny aware just how dangerous the drugs she was bringing into Bellewood were? Did she know the nicest boy at school, Mitchell Carmichael, had suffered an overdose and was likely still in a coma over it? Would she even care?

Sadie regretted her role in the most recent batch of Bliss coming through Bellewood, but she really hadn't understood what she was getting herself into. Even though Olivia had tried warning her.

With her phone in hand, Sadie searched Dante's online profile again. The request she'd sent was still pending. Surely he would have noticed it by now, but he still hadn't approved it. What a jerk. After the night they'd shared at the amusement park, the least he could do was acknowledge her existence.

These were the thoughts keeping Sadie up at night for the last several days. Those were the thoughts she chose to focus on anyway.

If she wasn't careful, a memory of her mother singing to her might creep in. This would only last a minute before remembering her mother was rotting underground for the last ten years, and could never sing again.

And if she still let her mind escape from her, memories of her father would slither in next. Her brilliant father and his raging madness. What he'd done to her. How he'd changed her.

She could still feel it, even now, if she focused hard enough, the needle he'd pierced her skin with. Absentminded, her head went to the night she wanted to forget the most.

A home in the woods, not a neighbor for miles.

A dark night, cloaked in sorrow and neglect.

A father gone mad, scary and unpredictable.

A young Sadie, with only a ragdoll for company, and not a soul to protect her.

If she was as strong as she was now, she could have stopped him. But she was only an average, motherless child then. Small and defenseless. Until his experiment made her deadly.

She remembered the torment of the days following the injection he'd forced on her when she was just nine years old. Like now, she couldn't sleep. But it was physical torment keeping her awake then.

Cold sweats.

Bloody nose.

Muscles that spasmed and burned, wanting to rip through her body.

A dangerous fever her father should have taken her to the hospital for. Of course, he hadn't.

He'd watched her. Studied her. He'd taken notes, even as she squirmed and shrieked, begging for relief that would not come. Screaming for him to help her.

When the pain finally went away, she'd slept. For a night, perhaps. Maybe days. And when she awoke a different person, they'd pretended nothing happened. But nothing was the same.

Her Dolly stayed on the floor where she'd dropped it the night before, untouched. She'd no longer cry herself to sleep, wishing for her mommy. She'd bury those memories of her instead.

And when something made her angry, there was hell to pay.

She was no longer the little girl who could be controlled. A bout of anger could lead to holes in the walls, a fit of rage might've ended in broken bones.

In these moments her father would sedate her, tempering the beast he himself had created.

So she'd learned to resent him. The strange, smart man who no longer scared her. She grew to pity him. The weak, sad fool.

With every passing year she'd grown stronger, less predictable. To the point that *he* was afraid of *her*. The very man that filled her nightmares when she was a girl, who had himself turned her into the beast of fury and rage she'd grown into. He could no longer handle her. He would no longer tolerate the violent outbursts at home that left him hiding in his room, even though she could have easily forced her way in if she'd pleased. The fights at school and ensuing expulsions that exhausted every school district within miles was the last straw. And her blatant disregard of trying to fit in as normal, even though he'd wanted her to, was what he hated most.

Even though it had all been his fault.

Bellewood had been the answer.

So she'd been sent off to a one bedroom apartment in a quiet seaside town to live in relative isolation with the meager savings he'd left her. A problem for somewhere else.

He was out of her life for good. Several months had passed since the last time she'd seen him, and she still would not let herself go there.

What if I had no choice? she thought with a shudder. *What if he was here in Bellewood? More disturbed than ever? What would I do then?*

She picked up her phone again, needing a distraction, and searched for Dante Nerosi. He still hadn't accepted her friend request.

Bastard.

\#

Later, as Sadie settled into bed for what promised to be another sleepless night, she heard a familiar rumbling in the distance, the sound of a powerful motor in a not-so-powerful car. That rumbling grew closer, until it was right outside her apartment and then stopped altogether.

Crap, Sadie thought, *how the hell does she know where I live?*

Sadie walked from her bed to her bedroom window which had a view of the front of the property. Sure enough, as expected, Destiny's purple Subaru was parked outside.

Destiny leapt out of the driver's side and Sadie opened her window to hear what she had to say.

"Get down here, we need to talk." Destiny's arms were crossed and Sadie could hear in her voice that whatever it was, it was important to Destiny.

After quickly dressing and popping in a piece of mint gum to disguise her expired breath, Sadie walked down to meet Destiny. Was this something to do with Bliss? Or was it about the other night when they almost kissed? Did she find out Sadie had hooked up with Dante and was upset about it?

"What the hell have you been telling Olivia?" Destiny demanded as soon as Sadie reached her.

"What do you mean?" Sadie asked, surprised at the question.

"She's been *stalking* my ass!"

"What the hell are you talking about?" Destiny was visibly upset, but she wasn't making sense. Olivia was *stalking* her?

"Her and that Ken-doll police officer—they followed me all the way to the warehouse earlier tonight."

"Olivia and Officer O'Brien?" Sadie asked, panicked, remembering the police officer Olivia had been talking to at the scene of Bree's murder. "They followed you and you led them to *the* warehouse?"

"I didn't know it was them! By the time I noticed someone was following me I was already way out of town, and I was scared, with a killer being on the loose and all! I drove to the warehouse for protection, thinking Jefe and them would take care of it if the killer was after me."

"Fuck...Fuckfuckfuck. So what happened? Do they know the drugs are coming through the warehouse? Do they know you're involved?" *Does Olivia know I got involved with it too?*

"Jefe was there and we gave them some BS story trying to throw them off. But they were asking *really* pointed questions, Sadie. What the hell did you tell them about me?"

"Nothing!" Sadie said. It wasn't a lie. She hadn't told Olivia what she'd done with Destiny the other night, but she didn't bother explaining that Olivia had already suspected Destiny's involvement before then.

"Well, now we're screwed." Destiny let out an exasperated sigh. "It's only a matter of time before the cops go back there with warrants. This won't end well, Sadie. Tell your friend to keep her nose out of shit that doesn't involve her or else she'll get hurt."

"Is that a threat?" Sadie demanded. Her whole body tensed, and she had to hold herself back from lashing out.

"Jefe and his people are dangerous, Sadie," Destiny explained. "Whatever happens, it won't end well. People, like your friend and her police officer boyfriend, could get killed if they go back there. Or if they're lucky, they'll win and we can all end up behind bars."

Shit, Sadie thought, defeated. She took a deep breath to settle her nerves. She was just beginning to like Bellewood. She didn't want to have to leave now.

"I'm gonna skip town for a bit, keep a low profile. You're welcome to join me."

"Like... Now?" Sadie asked, stunned.

"Would you rather wait for a warrant on your arrest? I just saw Dante and told him. He's packing his bags and will be leaving town for a bit too before shit really hits the fan. I think it's for the best, Sadie."

She was about to agree, to turn around and run up to her apartment to pack a bag and leave town with Destiny.

But *Olivia*. No. She couldn't leave. Not while her friend—and Olivia *was* her friend even if she wasn't speaking to her right now—was foolish enough to put herself in so much danger.

"I can't."

"Sadie—"

"No. Not right now. Not until I speak to Olivia." *And talk some sense into her.*

"I'm telling you, Sadie, that girl is bad news. Don't tell her anything!"

"Stop," Sadie said. "She's my best friend. I can't leave if there's a chance she could get hurt. I'll call her. I'll tell her to call this hunt off."

Sadie's phone rang. It was Olivia calling, as if she knew they'd just been talking about her.

CHAPTER TWENTY-ONE

"Olivia!" Sadie exclaimed when she answered the call, at once relieved that her friend was finally calling and scared at what she was going to say next. "Are you all right? Is everything OK?"

"I'm fine, Sadie," Olivia said, and Sadie breathed relief. "I'm still mad at you, but I had to talk to you."

Sadie walked a few steps to put some distance between her and Destiny, who was now glaring at her, annoyed she was speaking to Olivia.

"What's going on?"

"Remember Chad? The officer who was guarding the shore?"

"What about him?" Sadie asked, her eyes flicking to Destiny.

"We've been working together the last few days. That's part of the reason why I haven't reached out to you. I've been busy."

"And the other part of the reason you haven't been getting in touch with me?"

"You know why Sadie. I am so disappointed in you."

Hearing it hurt Sadie to her core, but she understood. She was disappointed in herself too. She should have stayed out of this whole mess.

"But it doesn't matter now," Olivia said. "This is way more important."

"What is it?" Sadie asked, knowing what Olivia would say next. Knowing she would mention Destiny, and the warehouse, and the Bliss. She wouldn't be surprised if she somehow found out that Sadie herself had gotten involved too.

"It's about Dante Nerosi," Olivia said, surprising her. Did she know Dante was involved in the drug ring?

"Chad told me that the police have zeroed in on him as a suspect in the Bellewood murders, Sadie. They're planning to arrest him."

"Dante?" Sadie felt unsteady on her feet, stumbling at the news. Sure, it was possible. Bree was found murdered surrounded by Bliss close to the amusement park where she'd hooked up with him, but... *No. I don't believe it.* "Why do the police suspect him?"

"Phone records. Dante had contact with both Katie and Bree shortly before they were murdered. Text messages suggest that he'd been intimate with both of them too. The one person Katie and Bree had in common was him."

Sadie saw red. Dante had had intimate relationships with both Katie and Bree? He'd never mentioned that. Of course. Because he had something to hide.

"I know you were interested in him after you met," Olivia said, "but you *need* to keep away from him, Sadie. Dante is dangerous."

Though Olivia warned her, she didn't even know the full extent of Sadie's relationship with Dante. She had no clue Sadie had been intimate with him too. Could Sadie have been his next victim?

No. A flash of her father deep in his madness flashed in her mind as she shook off the thought about Dante. She would never be anybody's victim ever again. As dangerous as Olivia thought Dante was, Sadie was far worse.

Before Olivia could warn her again, Sadie had disconnected the call and jumped into Destiny's car. "Take me to Dante."

CHAPTER TWENTY-TWO

Destiny knew the way to Dante's place well, as though she'd made the trip many times before.

"Are you going to tell me what this is about?" she asked when they reached their destination and parked her car. "What did Olivia say to you?"

For some reason Sadie had expected Dante to live in a mansion as opulent and sprawling as Brock's. While the house they were parked in front of was impressive, it was nowhere near what Sadie had envisioned. She found it amusing. Sadie tried to focus on the pointless observation, scared to let the gravity of what was happening settle in her mind. She could feel herself filling with an intensity she hadn't felt in a long time; she had to stay calm so she didn't freak out and lose all control.

Katie Phillips. Bree Huxley. Dante had killed them both?

"Wait in the car," Sadie said.

"What? Sadie, no! You're being weird. Tell me what Olivia said to you!"

"I will," Sadie said, *but I have to talk to Dante first.* "Just wait here. I won't be long."

She took off and made her way up Dante's drive, up the front steps of his porch, and then straight into his unlocked front door, as if she was a welcome guest that had been there before, and not the virtual stranger that she actually was to him.

No. Not a stranger. *We were intimate,* she reminded herself.

Dante had been intimate with Katie and Bree too, Olivia had told her. He'd been intimate with them shortly before killing them.

It could have been me. He was intimate with them *and he was intimate with* me *and he killed* them *and he could have killed* me.

Her thoughts were reeling. Her mind a blur. It made no sense. Nothing she was doing right now made any sense. She hated when she got like this. It all got so dark, so muddled, so confused. Lightheaded, her vision grew blurry, it was as if she was separating from her body.

Where is he?

She was searching his house and didn't even know it, her thoughts hazy.

She was vibrating again, skin tingling, teeth chattering as a coldness came over her. This always happened. No good ever came from it.

Where is he?

She walked up the stairs to the second floor of the house. Yes. She could smell him now. The smell of cheap cigarettes and his leather jacket. His bedroom must be near.

She could hear him moving around. In the bedroom around the corner.

He was intimate with me *and he was intimate with* THEM. *And then he killed them.*

Did *he kill them?*

Not Dante. He couldn't have. She knew him. She liked him so much. He couldn't have killed them. She trusted him. She had sex with him. But he was intimate with *them too.*

Sadie stood outside of Dante's Bedroom door. It was wide open, but his back was to her, so he had no idea she was watching. He piled clothes into an open suitcase.

Destiny had mentioned earlier that he was getting ready to leave before the drug operation blew up and everyone got arrested.

But was there more to it than that? Was he planning to leave because of what else he'd done?

Katie Phillips and Bree Huxley. *He was intimate with them and they died. He was intimate with them even though he was intimate with me.*

Katie and Bree.

And now another girl was in the picture. A gorgeous brunette walked toward him, her long legs accentuated further by the cut-off shorts she was wearing. She took a seat on his bed, settling into the covers like she slept there every night, like she owned the place.

Sadie didn't recognize her from school, and pegged her to be around Dante's age. She was beautiful, even though her big brown eyes displayed sadness as she curled her legs up into her chest watching Dante pack.

What is she doing here?

"Do you have to leave?" the young woman asked Dante, sounding forlorn.

"Just for a bit, babe," Dante said. "Only until things die down."

Why did he call her babe?

"But I don't want you to leave," she replied, her full lips forming a sad pout.

I hate her, Sadie thought venomously, her skin pulsing like live-wire.

Dante bent down to kiss her, and the whole world seemed to turn upside down.

That was all it took. Her oldest enemy had returned, and completely took over. Her closest friend. Her heart of fury.

Sadie was no longer in control of herself when she burst into the room. She couldn't stop herself even if she wanted to when she jumped on the girl, knocking her to the ground. A shocked Dante fell backward, powerless to protect her.

There was nothing he could do to stop Sadie.

There was nothing anyone could do when Sadie became like this, succumbing to the monster her father had created nine years ago.

All Dante could do was watch helplessly as Sadie killed the girl.

Savagely, the same way she had killed those other girls before, ripping into her chest and tearing out her heart, as if it was nothing. As if it was exactly what she deserved.

CHAPTER TWENTY-THREE

"Sadie, *what the Fuck!?*" Dante cried out as his girlfriend laid lifeless and bloodied on his bedroom floor.

"*You?*" he said, the sudden realization on his face as apparent as his repulsion. "*You* killed them?"

But the Sadie he had gotten to know wasn't there. She was someone else now. Someone as abnormal as she was terrifying, covered in blood, a vacant look in her angry eyes.

Dante sobbed, kneeled beside the young woman, trembling as he stroked her hair, soaked with blood.

Sadie drew closer as Dante stumbled to his feet, squaring up as though he could defend himself. She almost admired his bravery.

Dante was the first to throw a punch, landing square on her chin, but she barely felt it.

He hit her again and again, each time with more force. It didn't matter. Any injuries he inflicted would heal in seconds.

A pathetic desperation spread across his face as he tried to keep her at bay, walking backward until he cornered himself.

She pounced. He folded underneath her like he was nothing, his size and strength rendered useless under her preternatural force.

And even though the real her liked him so much, the monster inside her killed him.

You've given him so many chances, the voice inside of her cried out.

The same voice that filled her with hatred on the night when she'd followed him from the club where they'd first met. The night she saw him with Katie.

He can't be yours if he's with her, it had called, and so she followed. Katie never saw it coming. Neither did Sadie.

Dante should have been hers then.

For a while, he had been. The night at the amusement park was magical, it was Sadie's first time, and it was everything she imagined it would be. Dante was everything she imagined he would be. The real Sadie had been happy after that, high as she was. But the other Sadie was thrilled moreso. She was a creature of rage and passion, and Dante had satisfied that passion.

But she hadn't satisfied him.

After they'd had sex, Dante said he was going home. *Why does he need to leave? He should be with me.* But she couldn't let the anger show, she couldn't show him her other self. So she had hidden her feelings away and followed him in secret, disguised by the shadows around her.

He hadn't gone home like he said he would.

He's lying to you...

Sadie had followed him further to the beach next to the amusement park, where another young woman sat waiting for him: Bree Huxley.

Of all the girls at Bellewood Prep, why did it have to Bree? The same girl who stole Olivia's man had moved on to Sadie's.

No. She couldn't let Bree have him. She *wouldn't*.

Even though her skin burned and her vision was blurred at the edges with rage, she'd waited patiently. Watched as Dante and Bree took Bliss together, and then had sex. Just like he'd done with Sadie.

You deserve him more than she does...

Once they were done and Dante had left, Sadie struck Bree from behind, immediately knocking her unconscious. Then she couldn't help herself. She'd killed Bree like she'd killed Katie, disposed of her bloodied clothes, and went home. Only hours later did that furious monster within her settle, and when she awoke the next morning she had no memory of anything that had transpired.

She never remembered those violent outbursts, those sprees of savagery.

She wouldn't remember this either, killing Dante, when she came out of it.

Even though he laid beneath her in a pool of his own blood and a hole in his chest; even as his heart bled profusely in the hands that had torn him open, the innocent part of her would forget.

That innocent little girl that existed before her father had changed her *needed* to forget.

CHAPTER TWENTY-FOUR

"Sadie?"

She heard the familiar voice calling to her, but she couldn't respond.

She was in shock, sitting in the corner of the room amidst all her carnage, but she wasn't herself yet; the fury had not subsided.

"Dante?"

The voice was drawing closer.

It was Destiny, she realized.

She'd told her to stay in the car. *Why didn't she listen?*

"Where the hell are you guys?" Destiny called. "We need to go!"

Don't come up here, Sadie thought. *I can't let you see this. I can't leave any witnesses.*

She could hear Destiny coming up the stairs.

Fine, the monster acquiesced. That hateful part of her didn't care who had to die to keep her secret.

Destiny didn't deserve to die. She'd done nothing wrong. She was only ever kind to Sadie. Only caring.

There can be no witnesses.

But Destiny is innocent.

Sadie was coming to her senses. Her eyes darted across the room. *Where am I? What the* hell *is going on? So much blood. So much blood.*

"Sadie?" Destiny called again, closer this time.

"Destiny?" Sadie cried out, sobbing. "Destiny? I'm in here!"

She appeared in the doorway and when she took in the sight, a look of pure terror came over her. "What the FUCK?"

So much blood-shed. Dead bodies, too. Dante was among them.

"Destiny," Sadie shrieked-sobbed the name. "They're dead. They're both *dead*!"

"Oh my God, Sadie," Destiny's voice came out shaking, but she didn't cry, trying to stay strong for Sadie. She stepped over Dante's body, rushed to Sadie's side and helped her up. "What the hell happened?"

"Idon'tknowIdon'tknow. They're dead. They're both dead!"

Sadie was hysterical. She had every reason to be. Alone and surrounded by dead bodies, with no clue what happened.

"Why didn't you come for me?" Destiny said, leading Sadie out of the room and leaving the grizzly sight behind.

Sadie had no answers.

"Oh God, you poor thing, you're in shock, Sadie."

Of course she was. She'd just walked in on a massacre.

"We need to get out of here *now*."

"But D-Dante," Sadie stammered. "Dante and that girl."

"We can't help them now! I'm sorry Sadie, but we need to leave. I just got a call. The police have raided the warehouse and made a bunch of arrests. They're scouring all over town arresting anyone they think could be involved. They might be on their way here now."

"But Dante!" Sadie pleaded. They couldn't leave him like this.

"Oh shit!" Destiny cursed, realization striking her. "Whoever killed him probably wanted to get ahead of the police so that he didn't snitch! I told you there were some dangerous people involved in Bliss, Sadie. Oh God, I'm so sorry I ever got you into this mess."

They made their way outside the house and to Destiny's car. Destiny peeled the bloody clothes off Sadie's body. Sadie was still in too much shock to do so herself.

"We need to get you changed," Destiny said. She opened her car door, rummaged through a bag in the backseat, and emerged with fresh, clean clothes for Sadie to put on. "We can't draw any unwanted attention to us as we leave town. These clothes will have to do the trick until we can find you a shower."

Destiny led Sadie into the passenger seat, scrambled into the car next to her, and then they took off. Leaving the massacre, and Bellewood, behind them.

#

They drove through town and then through the Coquette Woods in silence until Destiny said a prayer to not be pulled over, and it was granted. Only hours later when they were well away from town did Destiny speak again, asking Sadie if she was all right and for more details of what happened.

Sadie didn't say a word. She couldn't if she wanted to. It was all so muddled for her. She hated when she felt like this. It happened too many times in the last nine years.

She didn't want to think about it. She didn't want to know what happened. What she'd seen. What she'd done.

It was easier to forget.

She was good at forgetting.

But she was still covered in blood, so she couldn't forget.

Not with Destiny next to her, reminding her, even now.

"It's okay," Destiny said at last, giving up. "You're still in shock. We'll talk about it when you're ready."

Would she ever be ready to speak about it? To do so would be admitting to herself what happened. She'd have to accept what she'd done.

In this confused space, it all started coming together.

Her father and his little experiment. The one that was meant to save her life, to heal her from the inherited illness her mother had died from. The experiment that had accidentally turned her into a monster. He'd spent years repenting for it, and trying to teach her to be normal, even though he'd made her this way.

He had no way of knowing how much worse she'd get. How she'd learn to hate him. He had no clue that the summer before her senior year would be her worst. And even though he feared her, he still loved her, and had no idea that she would end up killing him.

No. Sadie wouldn't think of this.

The memories of killing her father might send her over the edge again. Instead, she would forget. She would forget what she'd done to her father, and she would forget all she'd done in Bellewood. She was good at that.

It was lucky she had Destiny to take her somewhere new where she could start over.

Sadie was always good at starting over too.

The End

ACKNOWLEDGEMENTS

Thank you to my friends and family who encouraged and helped form this story. I'm forever grateful.

To Tony at Anuci Press. Thank you for taking a chance on me. I'm proud to be one of your authors.

To Katarina, my editor: Thank you for pushing me further and making this story better.

Thank you to Christy for the fire cover design!

Finally, thank You, my reader. I hope you enjoyed this story, and that you'll join me on the next one.

ABOUT THE AUTHOR

Andy Roo lives in Australia with his partner and their dog. 'Sadie's Lament' is his first (of many) books.